THE KNIGHT'S CODE

A TRAINING GUIDE

CONTENTS

Preface to the New Edition of *The Knight's Code*	5
Introduction to the Knights' Academy	9
The Knight's Code	10
The History of the Knight's Code	13
Welcome to the Knights' Academy	16
Academy Class Schedule	18
Code of Conduct	29
Course Materials Required	32
Disciplinary Actions	37
A Student's Daily Schedule	40
A Guide to Modern Weapons	45
The Knight's Code: Update	57
The Campus	58
Classes	68
Life at the Academy	76
The Squirebots	82
Academy Alumni	90
Conclusions	96

The Knight's Code: Digital Edition	**97**
When Powers Get Digital	**98**
NEXO Powers	**101**
Shields	**106**
HQ and Vehicles	**112**
Weapons	**140**
Jestro and The Book of Monsters	**152**
Fighting Tips	**166**
Hiding and Masking	**168**
Team Missions	**170**
Teamwork	**172**
What the Code Means to Me	**174**

PREFACE TO THE NEW EDITION OF *THE KNIGHT'S CODE*

BY THE CURRENT PRINCIPAL OF THE KNIGHTS' ACADEMY — SIR SWORDMORE BRICKLAND

The first edition of this noble book was written 500 years ago. For all this time, it has helped inspire and train generations of our kingdom's knights and heroes. An exact copy of the original Knight's Code text is printed in this book. Many at the Knights' Academy were reluctant to add anything to it, believing it had served us well for centuries. Why mess with success? But although the original Code written by our ancestors still remains at the core of our teaching, the world has changed dramatically over the past half a millennium, so we felt it was important to add further notes as a guide for the future knights of the Realm.

Foremost among these recent changes has been the advancement in magic and technology that has impacted our land. This new edition has an additional section starting on page 57 that will fully explain the technical, conceptual, and practical realities today's knights face.

Inspire? More like put to sleep.
—Lance

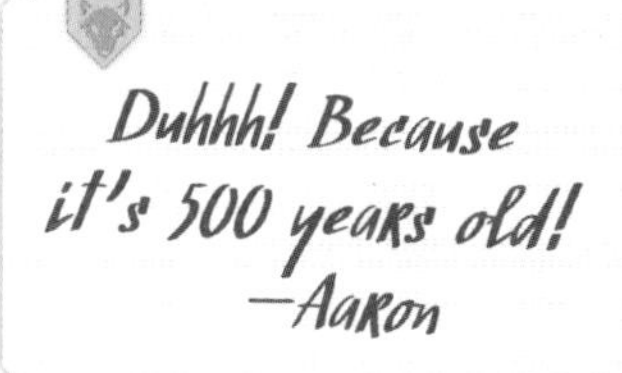

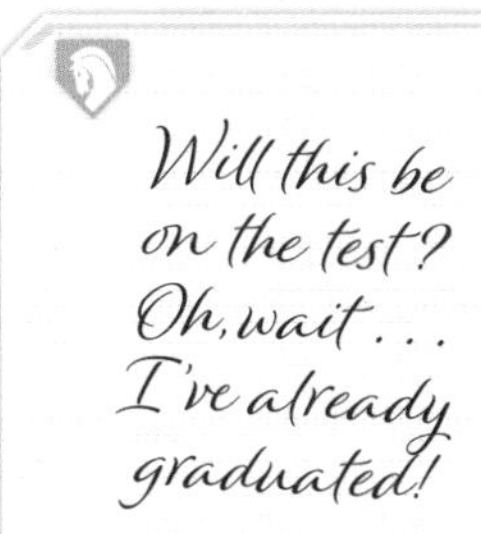

The Dark Ages called. It wants its textbook back.—Lance

CUT THAT OUT, LANCE! WE NEED TO HONOR THE BRAVE KNIGHTS WHO WENT BEFORE US AND LAID THE FOUNDATION FOR EVERYTHING WE DO. STOP DEFACING THIS BOOK WITH YOUR DIGI-NOTES. RESPECT.—CLAY

Uh . . . Clay . . . you do realize you're sticking notes in here, too.—Macy

Oops! She got ya there, Clay!—Aaron

BUT MINE ARE WORDS OF WISDOM . . . THAT JUST HAPPEN TO BE HANDWRITTEN. SO DON'T TREAT THESE PAGES AS SOMEWHERE YOU CAN STICK IN DOODLES OR SHOPPING LISTS.

Ooh! That reminds me: 24 eggs, 10 sticks of butter, 9 pounds ~~of sugar~~

—Axl

STOP THAT, AXL! I SAID ITS NOT SOMEWHERE TO STICK YOUR SHOPPING LISTS. JUST TURN THE PAGE AND READ THE REAL INTRODUCTION.

For
THE KINGDOM!

Check out that portrait of Merlok!
What . . . was he, like, ten years old back then? :/
MERLOK IS MORE THAN 500 YEARS OLD. AND THIS PART OF THE BOOK WAS ONLY WRITTEN 480 YEARS AGO. SO NO . . . HE IS NOT TEN.

INTRODUCTION TO THE KNIGHTS' ACADEMY

by Merlok

Welcome, ye aspiring knights, to the Knights' Academy—Knighton's training ground for protectors of the realm. In this academy you will learn many important subjects including history, combat, leadership skills, and professional conduct. But the most important thing you will learn is the Knight's Code.

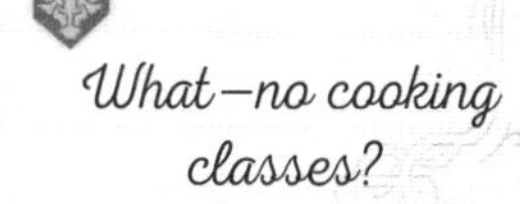

This Code shall govern your behavior and the day-to-day choices you make. It will see you through good times and those less certain. Refer to it often.

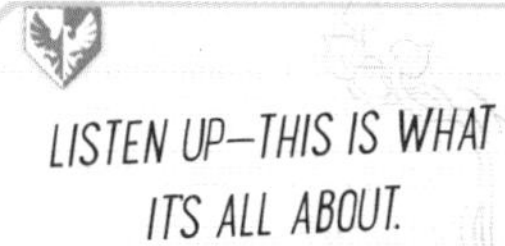

I am the academy's resident wizard. I recently replaced the legendary Gornzibarf the Great who held this position for nearly a thousand years and led the school through centuries of turmoil and triumph.

I ate too much chili last night and I almost GornziBARFED! Ha, ha, ha!

Yeah, if he was so great, why didn't he get himself a better name?

Let us embark on a journey magical and profound, where you shall learn how to be future protectors, leaders, and heroes, and how to be True Knights of the kingdom of Knighton.

Now get to class, students. The wonders of the kingdom await you.

The Knight's Code

A Knight is sworn to defend the weak, oppose the cruel, and protect their kingdom.

No cause is greater than ensuring the safety of that which a Knight is sworn to protect. A Knight must be brave, stand strong, face all dangers, and never give up.

All sworn duties under this Code shall be executed in a manner consistent with the Ancient Accords of Virtue and Chivalry, including its most profound pillars of Honor, Respect, Loyalty, Courage, Compassion, Diligence, and Justice.

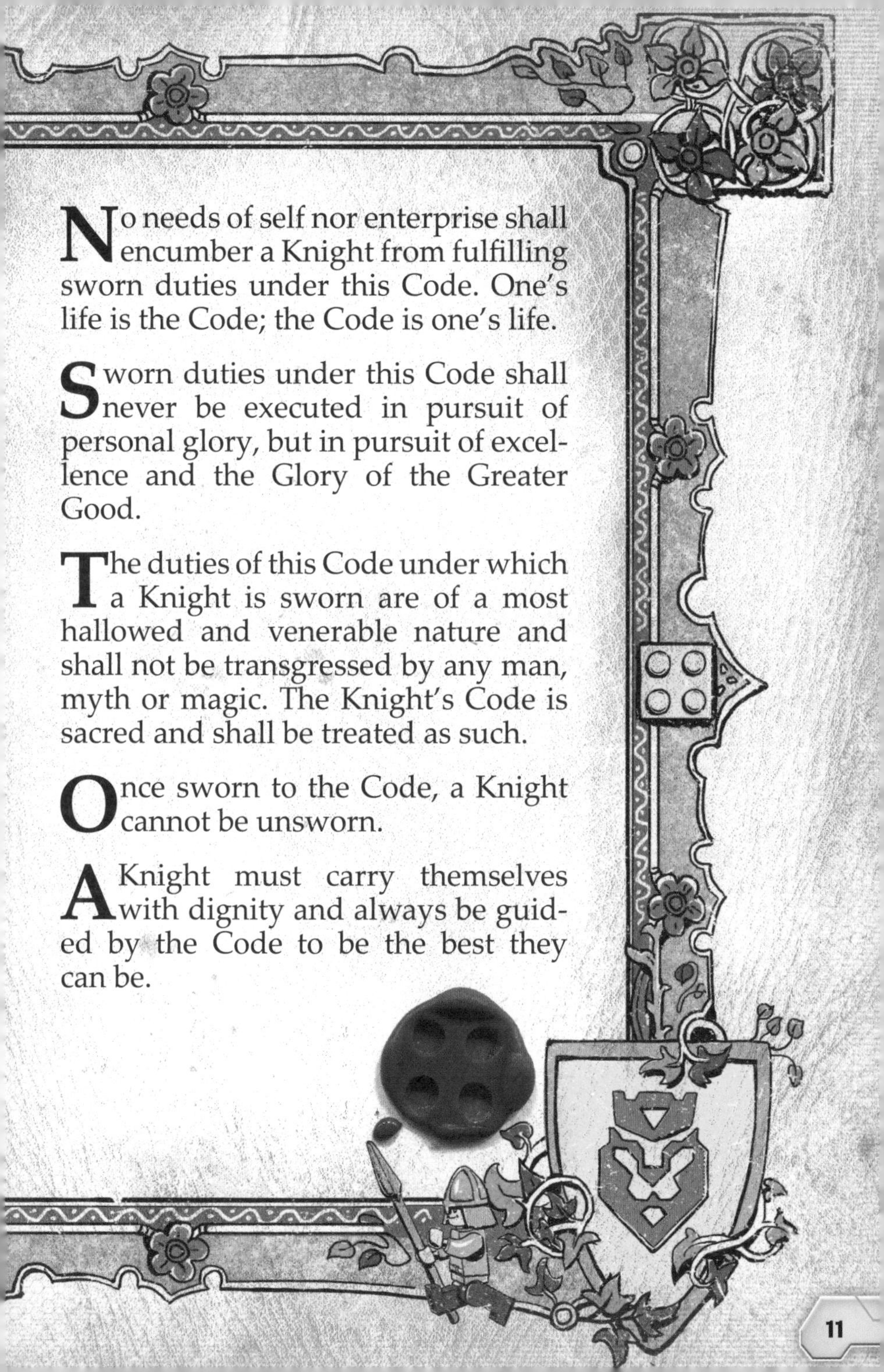

No needs of self nor enterprise shall encumber a Knight from fulfilling sworn duties under this Code. One's life is the Code; the Code is one's life.

Sworn duties under this Code shall never be executed in pursuit of personal glory, but in pursuit of excellence and the Glory of the Greater Good.

The duties of this Code under which a Knight is sworn are of a most hallowed and venerable nature and shall not be transgressed by any man, myth or magic. The Knight's Code is sacred and shall be treated as such.

Once sworn to the Code, a Knight cannot be unsworn.

A Knight must carry themselves with dignity and always be guided by the Code to be the best they can be.

THE HISTORY OF THE KNIGHT'S CODE

by Thunderblood Brickland—
Principal of the Knights' Academy

Is a "Swordmore" mightier than a "Thunderblood"?

What will the next principal's name be? Lightningveins! :>

The Code of the Knighthood of Knighton (aka "The Knight's Code") was inscribed more than a thousand years ago on a sun-cured dragon skin by the Order of the Eight—the first and most famous protectors of the land now known as Knighton. A copy of that original skin can be seen on the previous pages.

Just prior to the creation of the Code, the Realm was a lawless wasteland ravaged by dragons, monsters, and evil creatures of all kinds.

Sounds like my kind of place! B-)

A local farmer named Augustin Halbert gathered seven of the bravest, strongest, and most interesting citizens he could find to fight back against the evil that ruled the world around him.

Augustin is my great-great-great-etc., grandfather! He's on one of my favorite tapestries at the castle.

It was a long and valiant struggle, but eventually the eight self-taught warriors found victory over their much more powerful opponents. The eight believed that their success was not just based on their superior intelligence and battle skills, but on something more intangible; a type of honor, loyalty, and bravery that bound them together. They wanted to explain this unspoken "code" to all the protectors of the realm who would follow in their stead.

AND I THANK THOSE EIGHT EVERY DAY FOR WHAT THEY DID!

He-he! He said, "Brownwater." :))

Following their final victory over the Brownwater Brood of the Badlands, Halbert asked each of the seven warriors to come up with one statement or command that most effectively expressed their best behavior and conduct. These eight statements—one from each knight—became the Code of the Knighthood of Knighton, also known as the Knight's Code.

Aspiring knights have studied the Code and followed it for centuries. Even today, it is one of the most important documents studied and learned at this academy.

By the way, I still don't know it.

Yes, we know. :P

Most of the Order of the Eight went on to become the Founders of Knighton. Augustin Halbert became Knighton's first king (his family still sits on the throne). Valiant warrior Reginald Brickland started the institution that became the Knights' Academy. And Therence "The Feathersword" Richmond—a bird catcher who became an effective warrior—founded the town of Auremville. His family became one of the wealthiest in the kingdom.

They called your ancestor FeatherSword?

Yeah! Feathers were really tough in the old days.

What, did he tickle his opponents to death?

I like catching birds! Especially . . . fried chickens!

WILL YOU GUYS PLEASE TAKE THIS SERIOUSLY?

WELCOME TO THE KNIGHTS' ACADEMY

Can you believe this guy is related to our headmaster, Brickland?

I can totally see the resemblance— Helmet Hair!

Wait . . . are we talking about the same Knights' Academy that I went to? :-/

Nah, this part of the book was written, like 500 years ago. Ignore it.

WHAT? THIS IS ESSENTIAL READING. PAY ATTENTION! :X

Now that you students have studied, memorized, and dedicated your life to the Knight's Code, it is time for you to become better acquainted with the dawn-to-dusk training, studying, and uncompromising commitment to the pursuit of greatness that will be your next four years here at the Knights' Academy. As a direct descendant of the Great Reginald Brickland, one of the founders and creators of the Knight's Code and this Knights' Academy, I, Thunderblood Brickland,

No way! Is that his real name? :-O

have dedicated my life to turning you meek and helpless little children into great knights and protectors of the realm. You may struggle at times. You may struggle and suffer at times. You may even ask yourself, "Am I strong enough . . . am I smart enough . . . am I noble enough to be a True Knight?" But always remember this: Bricks in a bundle are unbreakable.

You will learn much in your time here at the academy. Most importantly, you will learn that a castle is only as strong as its weakest brick. And you shall, as knights of Knighton, become the strongest, smartest, and most noble bricks the realm has ever known. This shall be your mission, your duty, and your life's work. In a few short years, you will become Knights of Knighton. Or, as I like to say, "the bricks that guard our land."

Good luck, students!
Your kingdom awaits its protectors.

Thunderblood Brickland

Knights' Academy Principal

For the record, I was NEVER little. ;))

I'm suffering now just reading this. :(

YES. YES AND YES! =D

Uh . . . Are we building castles here or learning how to become knights? I'm confused.

I think he just likes to talk about bricks because his name is BRICKland. ;)

ACADEMY CLASS SCHEDULE

BEST. FOUR. YEARS. EVER.

All students at the Knights' Academy are expected to complete their studies and training over four years of intensive academic and physical education. Each year focuses on a different aspect of your knight's training. Here is what you can expect in your extremely demanding and unforgiving time at the Knights' Academy.

Oh, please . . . It wasn't that bad.

Novice? More like "total newbie!" ;P

YEAR ONE – NOVICE

Introduction to the Knight's Code: Basics of Knighthood

Chivalry and Ethics 101

Is it bad if you cheat on your ethics test? ;)

**Combat Skills—
Level 1:
Swords and Axes**

**Beginner's
Metallurgy and
Protective Armor**

**Introduction
to Equestrian
Skills and
Horsemanship**

If it looks like a horse and hovers—I am ON it!

Uh, this part of the book is so old—these were actual real horses . . . with legs.

Ewww! Gross!

**Castle Economics
(elective)**

**Creative Tapestry
Making (elective)**

YEAR TWO – APPRENTICE

The History of Knighton

What . . . no digi-arrows? Dude, this is so medieval!

Combat Skills—Level 2: Bowmanship and Range Weapons

Chivalry Honors

Advanced Metallurgy and Protective Armor

Advanced Horsemanship and Jousting

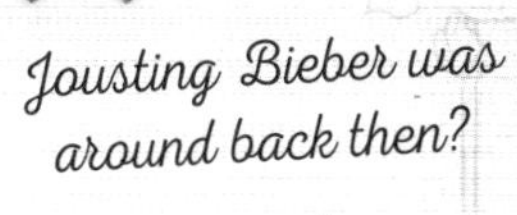

Jousting Bieber was around back then?

Er, you're kidding, right? :-/

Technology (from alchemy to magic)

Huh? That's the "technology" class? :-?

Physical Education

Horse Cart Shop (elective)

What's a "horse cart"?

Woodwork and Forest Monsters (elective)

YEAR THREE - WEAPON BEARER

Geography of Knighton

Combat Skills— Level 3: Battlefield and Siege Tactics

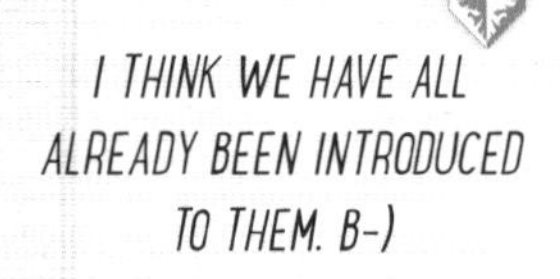

Introduction to Monsters (lab, plus field work)

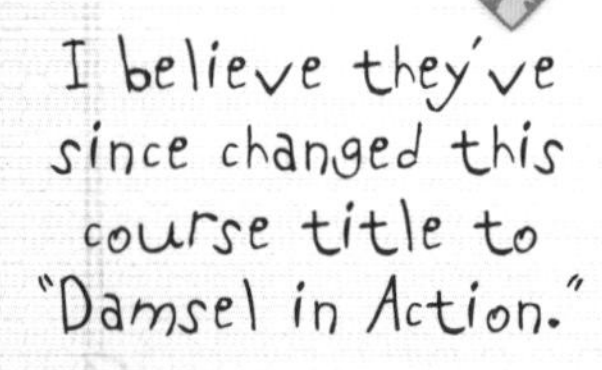

Damsel in Distress 101

Foreign Language—choose from: Latin, French, Monster Growl

I'm a master in Monster Growl: eRRRR, aghRRR, bllll ;P

First Aid 101—from leeches to dried toads

OK, seriously? Is that the best "medicine" they had? :-O

Physical Education

Ballroom Dancing (elective)

THIS IS AN ELECTIVE? THAT'S OPEN FOR DEBATE. HA. HA. HA!

Wait . . . did Clay just make a joke? ;))

Diplomacy/Debate (elective)

YEAR FOUR – SQUIRE

Combat Skills— Level 4: Prolonged Military Campaigns and Battles

Advanced Monsters (prerequisites: Combat 3, First Aid 101)

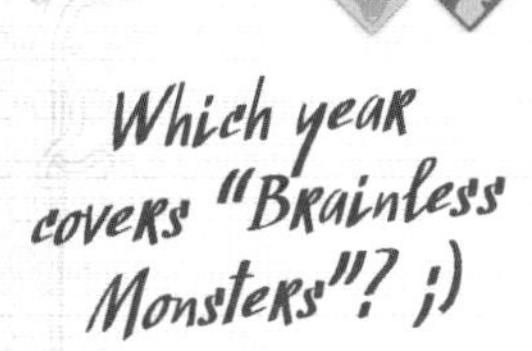

History of the Royal Families of Knighton

Believe it or not, I only got a B in this. :-/

Field Study (students must go on a quest)

Posing Heroically

Ha! I could've taught this class!

Modern Ballistics and Machines (Is the catapult the weapon of the future?)

No.

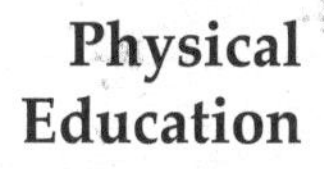

Physical Education

Legend Building (elective)

My legend was already built. B-)

Pottery and Ceramics (elective)

Ooh! My favorite! :))

Sweet shields! :))

Yeah,
but can they get
a digi-download?
The answer is no.

THEY DIDN'T NEED
DOWNLOADS OF NEXO
POWERS BACK THEN.
BUT WE DEFINITELY
NEED THEM NOW. :)

GRADUATION – SHIELD BEARER

Upon completion of all the required courses and one elective in each year of enrollment, students will receive the Knights' Academy Degree of Knighthood. Graduates will also be awarded their Knight's Shields and become Official Protectors of the Realm.

Did I ever
tell you how much
I liked my Pottery
and Ceramics class?
I drew a picture of
one of the coffee mugs
I made. :))

CODE OF CONDUCT

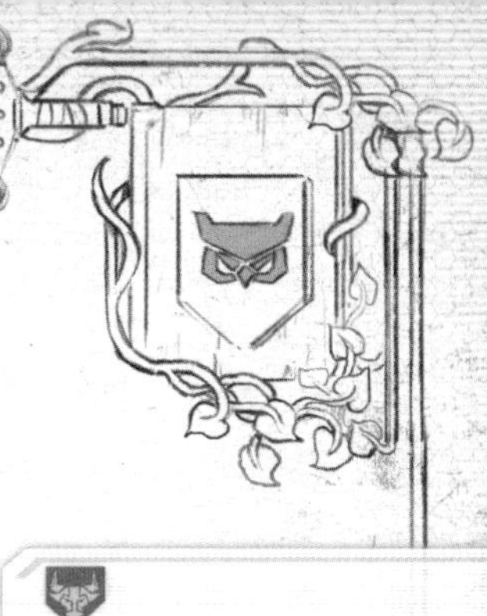

Enrollment in the Knights' Academy is considered one of the highest privileges granted to the youth of Knighton. You have been chosen to be future protectors of the Realm, saviors of all that is worth saving. You are the next generation of the Knights of Knighton. As such, you will be expected to conduct yourselves in accordance with the principles set forth below.

I just got a coupon for "One free ice cream" from Sir Scoopsalot's shop. Now that's a privilege.

You will always follow the Knight's Code and apply its guidance to all decisions and actions pursued while at the academy.

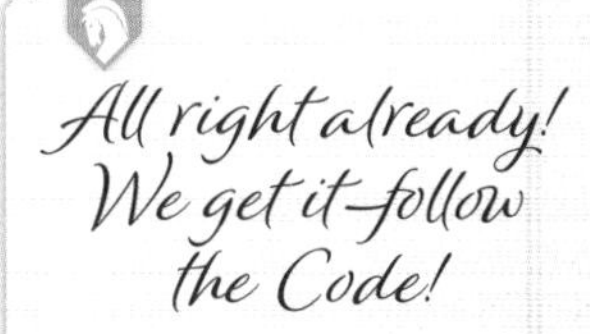

You will always seek justice, fairness, and safety for the king and the kingdom of Knighton.

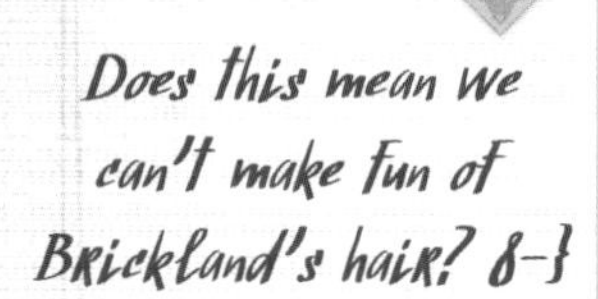

You will show <u>appropriate deference and respect</u> to all the teachers and administrators of the Knights' Academy.

You shall also treat your fellow students with respect and fairness. All are equal at the Knights' Academy.

Ah, that's easy. I just wipe my armor down with my underpants! :))

That is so totally not appropriate. :/

It's not? Oh . . . I'd better let Lance know then. He paid me to clean his armor, too.

What? AHHHH!

Armor shall be <u>polished regularly</u> using appropriate cleaning and shining agents.

Fraternizing with monsters or evildoers of any kind is <u>strictly forbidden</u>.

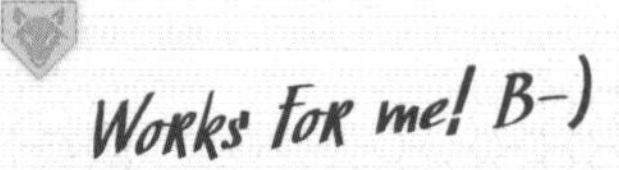

Recreational belching, gulping, snorting, and/or farting is strictly prohibited. As per the Fox Rule, no exceptions are allowed.

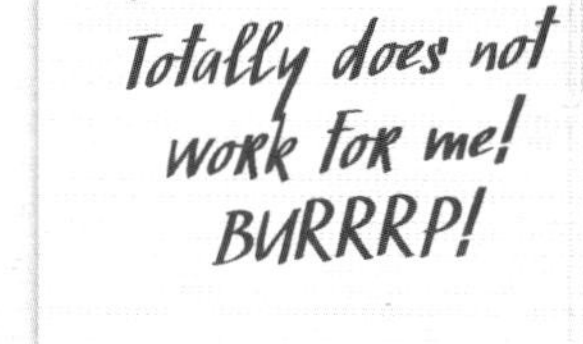

Totally does not work for me! BURRRP!

All meals shall be consumed in the dining hall during dining hours, unless one can prove a demonstrated need for additional nutrition.

Where do I get a doctor's note for this? :-/

Any infractions of this code shall result in a student receiving a demerit on his/her permanent record.

Keep this book and its contents secret. Share its contents with no one.

But how are we supposed to keep this secret? /:)

Like this: "Hey, if you're reading this right now and you're not a knight, raise your hand." Hmm . . . I don't see anyone raising their hand. So we're all good. B-)

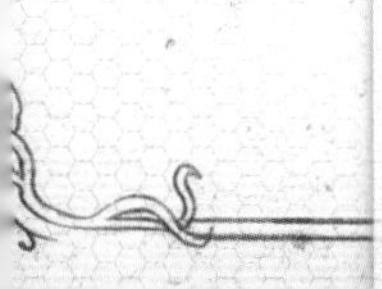

LOOK AT THIS LIST: NO NOTEBOOKS. NO COMPUTERS. NO INSTANT DOWNLOADS. NOW THAT REALLY IS "OLD SCHOOL"!

No, this was nuts! The old days were soooo lame.

COURSE MATERIALS REQUIRED

Attendance at the Knights' Academy requires all students to come to class prepared with one or more of the following materials:

6 rolls of parchment or properly cured animal skin to be used for taking notes

What if the feather quill is still attached to the bird? Will that be OK?

2 sharpened quills made of bird feathers (duck or goose preferred)

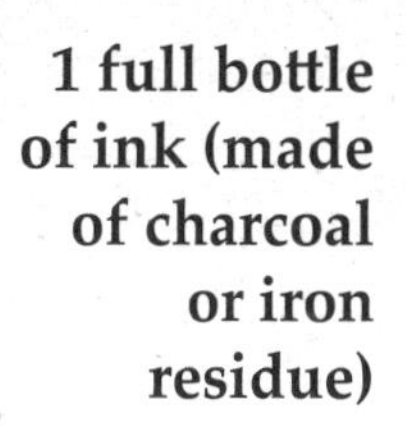

1 full bottle of ink (made of charcoal or iron residue)

30 pieces of coal for the classroom furnace

Seriously? No central heating?

3 separate servings of gruel (1 lunch portion, 2 snack sized)

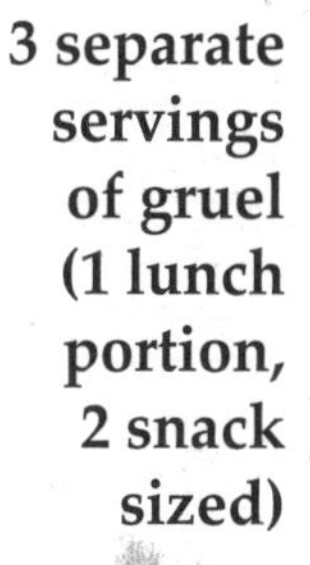

I see the words "lunch" and "snack," but what's this "gruel" stuff? :-/

1 complete set of chain mail and armor (for combat classes only)

It'd be pretty funny to wear your armor to art class.

Or to ballroom dancing. <:-P

BORRRRing! |-)

1 practice sword (wooden)

NOW WE'RE TALKING! :))

1 broadsword (iron)

You don't get your real shield until you graduate . . . or in my case, until your father—the King—says it's OK.

1 apprentice shield

And that dummy's name is Clay! Ha! Just kidding, Clay.

1 combat practice dummy

Additional combat tools and armaments as required by class curriculum

I BRING EVERYTHING WITH ME. JUST IN CASE. :)

Yes . . . we know . . .

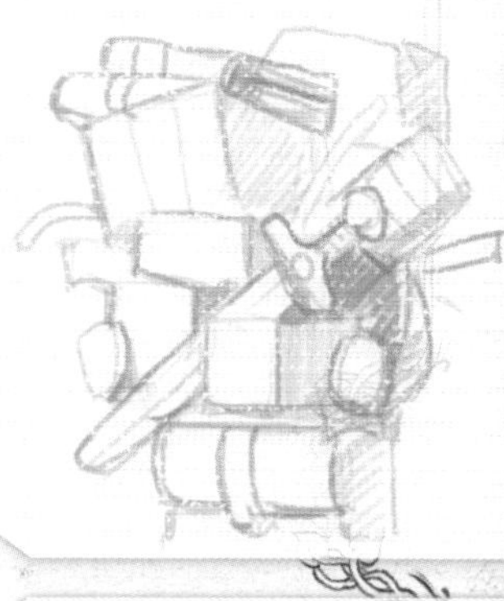

In addition, proper classroom attire is required at all times, including woolen trousers, horsehair cloak, animal skin shirt, and tunic. The student is responsible for obtaining all class materials from the appropriate merchants, blacksmiths, and/or alchemists. Failing to obtain any of the above items for the appropriate class shall result in disciplinary action. No excuses will be accepted.

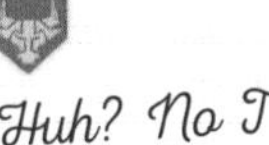

Huh? No T-shirts? :-/

Oh, c'mon . . . how about this excuse: "My combat dummy was so dumb he got lost on the way to class!"

"The dog ate my parchment!"

"SORRY, I'm not dRessed pRopeRly, but my 'tunic' was 'out of tune!'" Ha, ha, ha, ha! :P

GUYS. THEY WERE SERIOUS BACK THEN . . . TURN THE PAGE!

DISCIPLINARY ACTIONS

A True Knight *always* does the right thing without fail and without statutory decree. Students who are *studying* to be knights, however, sometimes need to be reminded of their proper duties and responsibilities under the rules of the Knights' Academy. Failure to follow any of the rules shall result in disciplinary action, ranging from a minor tickling to a prolonged stay in the academy's dungeon. In addition, rule infractions shall result in one demerit being added to a student's permanent record. The accumulation of three demerits shall result in a scroll from the principal being sent home to a student's guardian by carrier pigeon or horse messenger.

WHAT?
Are they serious?

They were pretty strict back then. Things were a lot more relaxed by the time we got there.

What? No email? :-O

Oh, come on! Dude, if they still did that when we were there, they would've renamed the dungeon "Aaron's Bedroom."

The accumulation of five or more demerits on a student's permanent record shall result in the student being assigned detention in the academy's dungeon for a minimum of fifteen days. Recurring infractions shall result in detention, suspension, and/or ninety days chained up in the academy's dungeon with only salted mud to eat for breakfast, lunch, and dinner.

WELL. AT LEAST YOU GET THREE MEALS.

Yum . . . Salted mud . . . 8->

Sample infractions liable to incur a demerit include:

- **Failure to complete all schoolwork or homework**
- **Failure to bring sufficient course materials to class or field work**
- **Failure to respect the academy staff or faculty**
- **Failure to memorize and fulfill the Knight's Code**

Yep, I've probably done all of that and more.

Check, check, check, and check! :-)

In addition, attendance is mandatory at all classes and after-school functions. There are only three acceptable excuses for failing to attend any of the academy's scheduled events. These include . . .

You are incapacitated due to a severe case of the plague

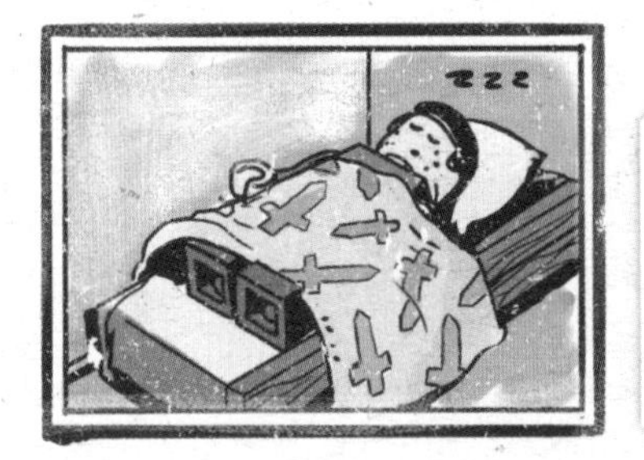

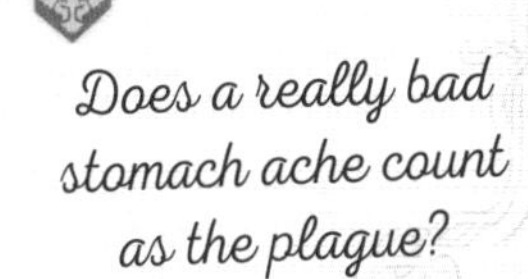

You have been eaten by a dragon

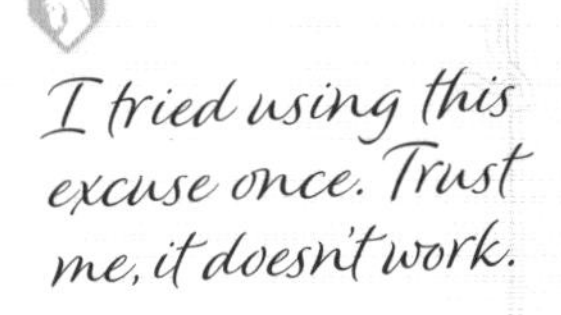

You have an excuse from the king

Of course, I would NEVER ask my father to write me an excuse. Tee-hee-hee!

A STUDENT'S DAILY SCHEDULE

What? No digitally monitored goose feather mattress? This isn't school! It's torture!

I bet they spent all day scratching their bottoms!

GUESS THEY HAD NO INDOOR PLUMBING. :-/

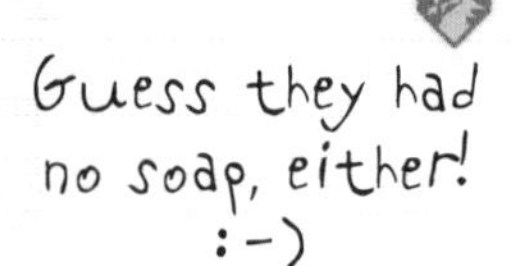

4 a.m.
Wake up, get out of a bed made of <u>solid wood and straw</u>.

4 – 4:30 a.m.
<u>Remove bed splinters from back</u> and clean extra straw pieces out of underwear.

4:30 – 5 a.m.
<u>Retrieve water from well for shower.</u>

5 – 6 a.m.
Start fire and heat water for shower.

6 – 6:05 a.m.
Take shower; wash skins with <u>soft rocks and butterfat.</u>

6:05 – 7 a.m.
Avoid insects attracted by smell of butterfat on your skin.

7 – 8 a.m.
Milk cows, collect eggs, pick bugs out of porridge.

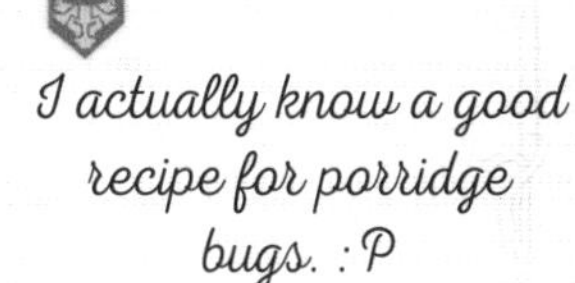

I actually know a good recipe for porridge bugs. : P

8 – 8:30 a.m.
Eat breakfast.

8:30 – 11 a.m.
Castle chores—cleaning and scrubbing the castle and removing the principal's scabs and ingrown toenails.

I believe I speak for all of us when I say: Ewwwwww!

11 a.m. – 1:30 p.m.
Hunt for lunch.

1:30 – 2 p.m.
Start fire for lunch.

2 – 2:30 p.m.
Cook and eat lunch hunted that morning.

2:30 – 3 p.m.
Attend classes in knight-related subjects.

Dudes, are there only thirty minutes of classes a day?

YES. AS A MATTER OF FACT. JUST SURVIVING IN THOSE DAYS WAS SO CHALLENGING. THERE WASN'T MUCH TIME FOR CLASSES.

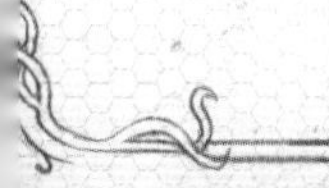

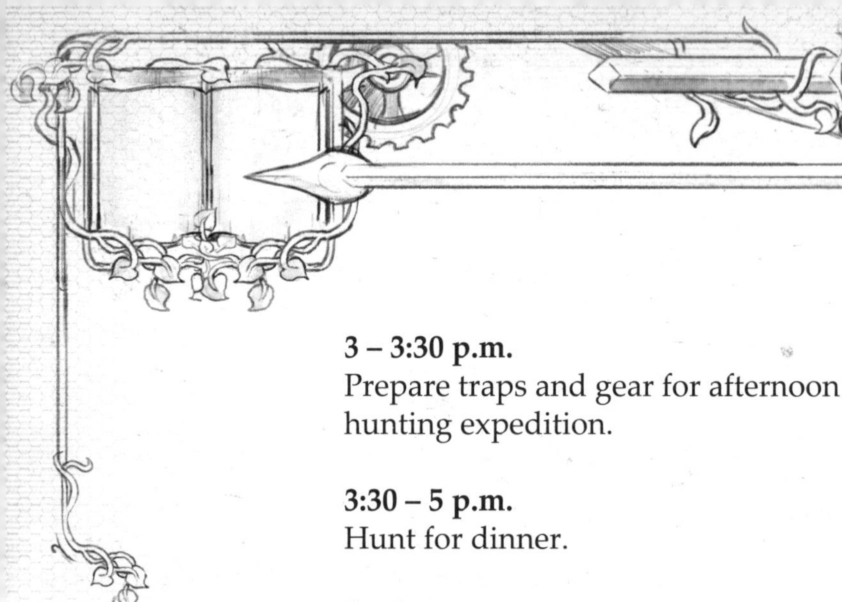

3 – 3:30 p.m.
Prepare traps and gear for afternoon hunting expedition.

3:30 – 5 p.m.
Hunt for dinner.

5 – 6 p.m.
Prepare dinner with other knights.

THATS FROM EATING IMPROPERLY PREPARED AND STORED FOOD PRODUCTS.

6 – 7 p.m.
Deal with stomachache.

7 – 8 p.m.
Have it treated by in-house doctor, who can prescribe leeches and bloodletting for stomachache.

I actually know a good recipe for leeches, too! :))

8 – 8:05 p.m.
Homework

Five minutes of homework? Old Times Rule!

8:05 – 9 p.m.
Finish castle chores, including scrubbing of principal's bedpan.

9 – 10 p.m.
Extra credit courses—for those students hoping to graduate the academy on time.

10 – 10:30 p.m.
Gather more straw for straw bed.

10:30 p.m. – 4 a.m.
Sleep if you have completed all your chores and/or survived.

Prepare for more bottom scratching, too! :))

I have to say . . . I'm glad we didn't go to the academy back then. :-|

Me too!

Not me. Barely any classes, just hunting and sleeping! Woo-hoo! Bring on the butterfat showers!

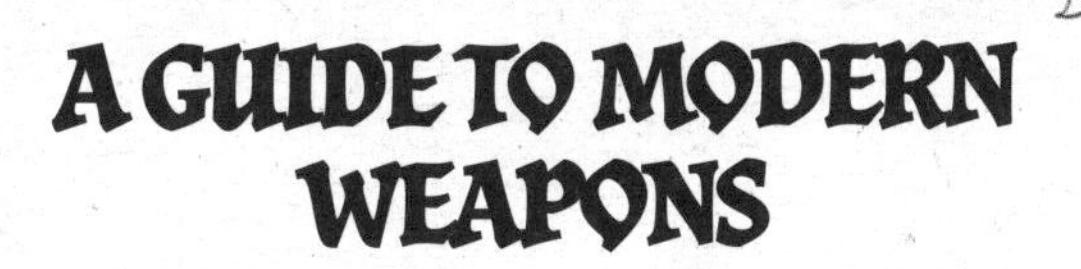

A GUIDE TO MODERN WEAPONS

As a student at the Knights' Academy, you will have access to the most modern weapons available in the kingdom today. We have had a team of blacksmiths and alchemists working around the sundial to build you some of the most advanced defensive and offensive implements. Prepare to be wowed, young apprentice. This is the future of battle.

FOR REAL? A CHILD KNOWS HOW TO MAKE THOSE. :D

THE SWORD

One of a knight's main tools of combat is the sword, which can be used to both strike an opponent and deflect an opponent's attack.

Below you will find a diagram pinpointing the many important parts of the sword and how our experts here at the Knights' Academy have improved upon them.

THE BLADE—For many years, the cutting/thrusting part of the sword was made of copper, iron, or even very sharp rocks. But our weapon smiths have begun building swords with a revolutionary new material called steel. It is stronger, lighter, and more durable.

They just figured out what steel blade is? Ughhhh . . .

THE CROSS GUARD—Defines the end of the blade and the beginning of the grip; used to protect a knight's hand in battle.

IF ONLY IT COULD HAVE DOWNLOADED NEXO POWERS LIKE MY CLAYMORE SWORD.

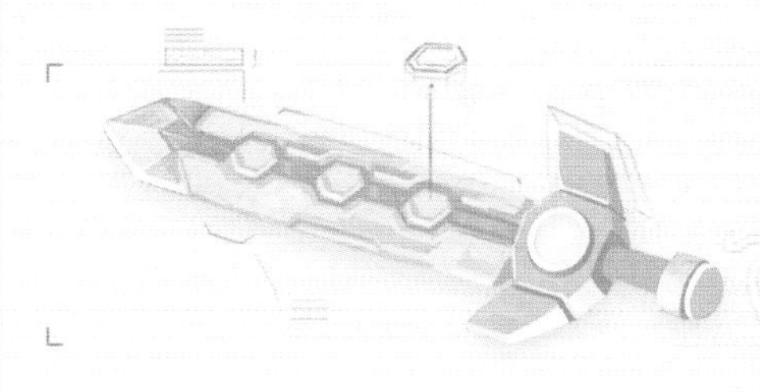

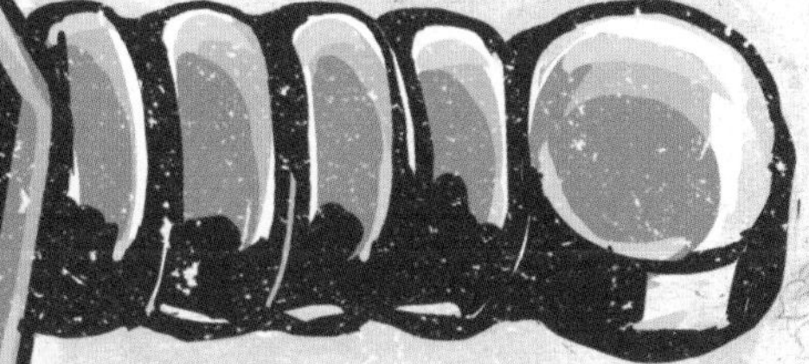

THE GRIP—New advancements in fabric-making have allowed us to cover the handle of the sword with a protective material. Until recently, the grip was sharp and metal like the blade, and this had a severely adverse impact on the user's hand and fingers . . . if one had any left.

Yikes! How long did it take them to work it out?

I'm counting the years—on my fingers, which I still have!

ARMOR

Some of our most notable advancements in the world of combat technology have to do with reducing the weight of the armor our knights wear. We have succeeded in lowering its bulk from nearly 300 pounds to just over 200 pounds. Yes, the armor still weighs more than your average adult wearing it, but at least no future knights will get hopelessly stuck in place during battle.

HELMET—Previous efforts to protect one's head with coconut shells have been replaced by the metal helmet. Coming in at a weight of only seventy-five pounds, it will compress the average user's neck like an accordion within two hours of continuous wear. But at least the warrior's face will be safe.

Whew! That's a relief. I like my face.

Yum . . . coconuts . . . 8->

BREASTPLATE—This area has been reinforced with both steel and concrete to protect the chest.

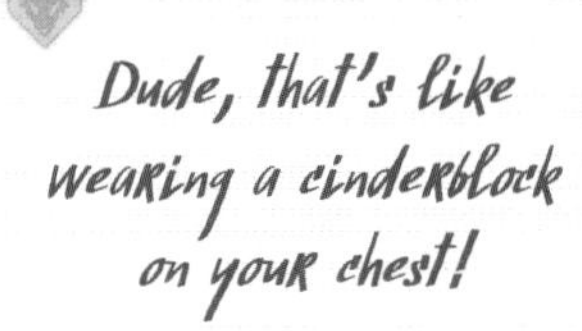

GAUNTLETS—These actually do nothing, but our fashion-forward armor designer insisted that they tie the whole ensemble together.

ARMORED LEGGINGS—Leggings are still heavy and unwieldy. However, advancements now allow knights to bend their knees almost five degrees. It's not quite enough to allow a knight to walk properly, but it comes in handy if you need to step over a small rock.

Look out, small rocks! We're coming for you!

Are they serious? A knight's crest represents family and kingdom! :-/

Sorry, Macy, I have to agree—if the shield can't fly, it's totally useless.

With my shield I can actually serve those snacks and microwave them at the same time! :P

A KNIGHTS SHIELD AND CREST ARE ALMOST AS IMPORTANT AS THE CODE AND FOLLOWING ITS RULES. THEY ARE ONE'S PRIDE, PROTECTION, AND SIGN OF UNITY.

THE SHIELD

This is a mostly useless piece of armor, and will never play any significant role in a knight's duty. The chief purpose of the shield is to hide any flaws and rust spots in the body armor. It is extremely demoralizing to walk onto the battlefield with an unsightly scuff or tarnish on one's breastplate. The most you can ever hope to do with your shield is hang it on a wall or serve your friends dinner snacks on it.

FRONT OF SHIELD—Nothing to see here except maybe some crests or other doodles used to distract an opponent.

BACK OF SHIELD—Even less to see here. This is where you hold it.

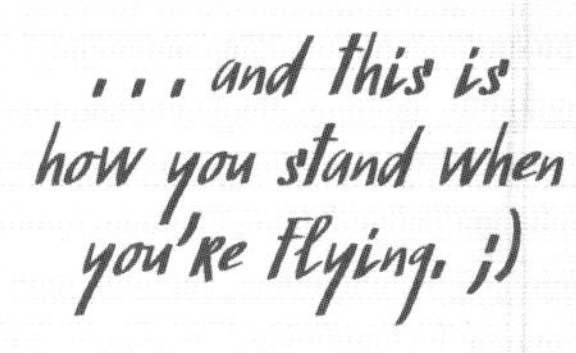

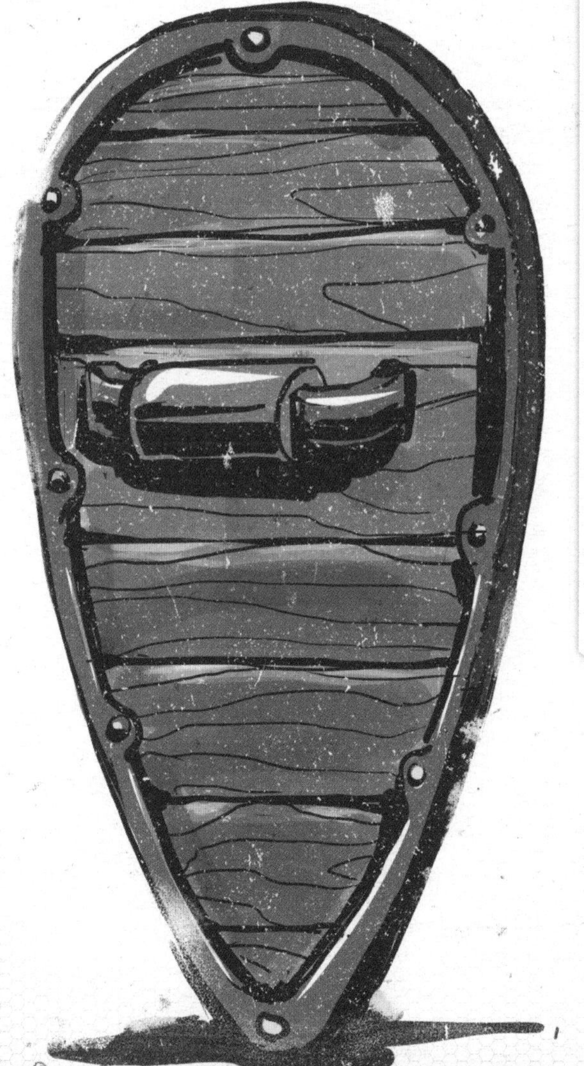

THE LIMB—This is a highly elastic piece of material that used to be made of goat horns. But the academy's weapon smiths now use a type of treated birchwood or elm.

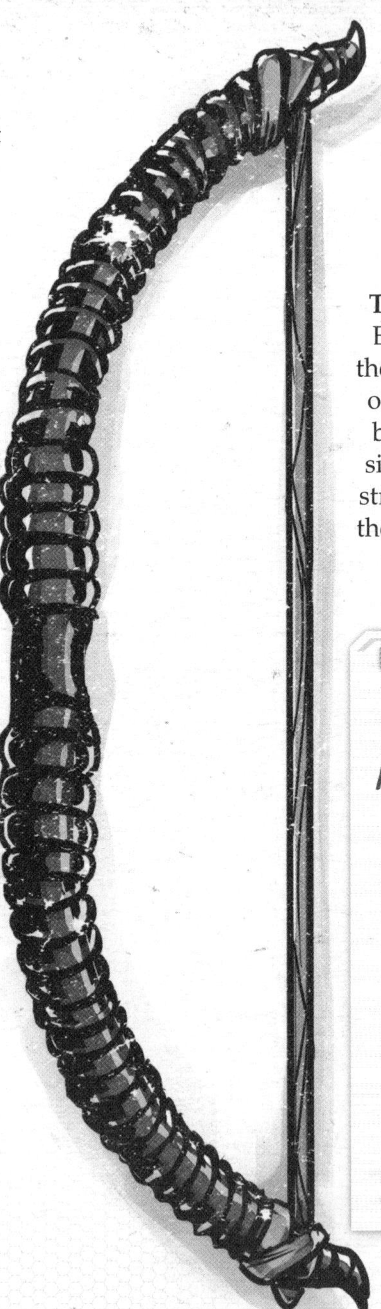

THE STRING—Earlier versions of the string were made of celery fibers and beeswax. We have since improved our string by reinforcing the celery fibers with toad spit.

Bet the goats are really happy about that. :)

No way, dudes! If I find any toad spit on my bow, I'm switching to a sword!

THE BOW AND ARROW

The projectile weapon is a relatively new achievement in the world of modern combat. One of the main expressions of this combat tool is the bow and arrow. Again, our weaponsmiths have been working hard to improve this newfangled device.

Modern? :)

THE ARROW—Now nearly ninety percent of our arrows are almost straight. The other ten percent, well . . . three students last year ended up shooting themselves in the rear with their own arrows.

Only three? They must have been really good. :P

THE ARROWHEAD—Large rocks have been replaced with sleek, polished blades. We've attached these blades to the shafts with that same toad spit we used on the strings, but they don't stay on very well. This is very much a work in progress.

I think I'd rather be a damsel in distress than an archer in those days!

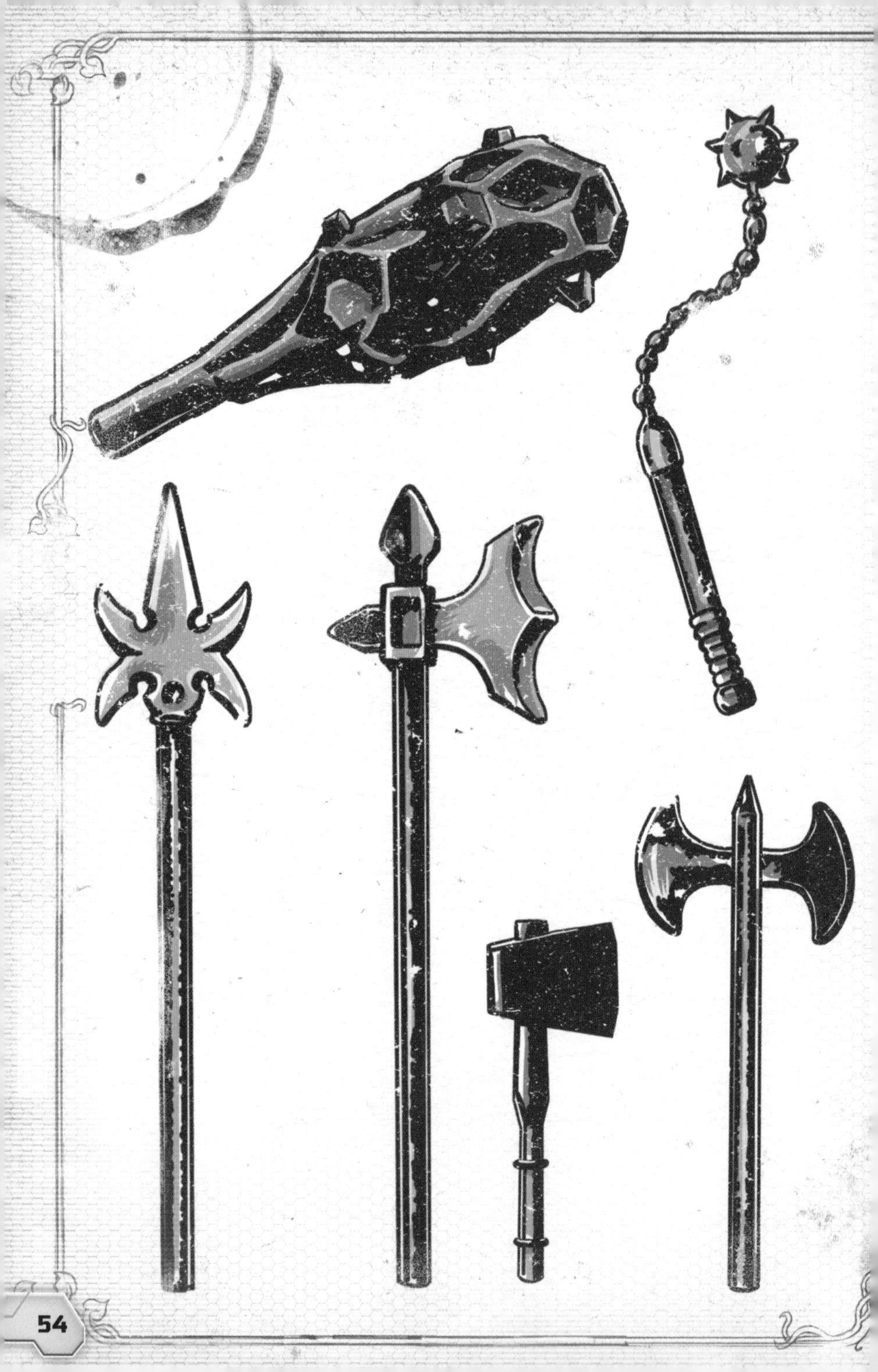

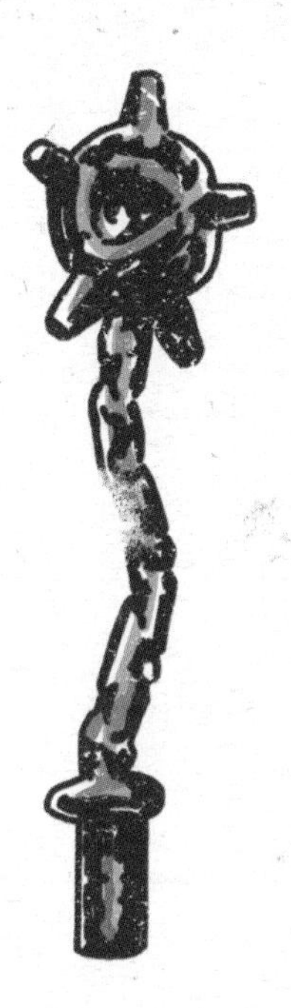

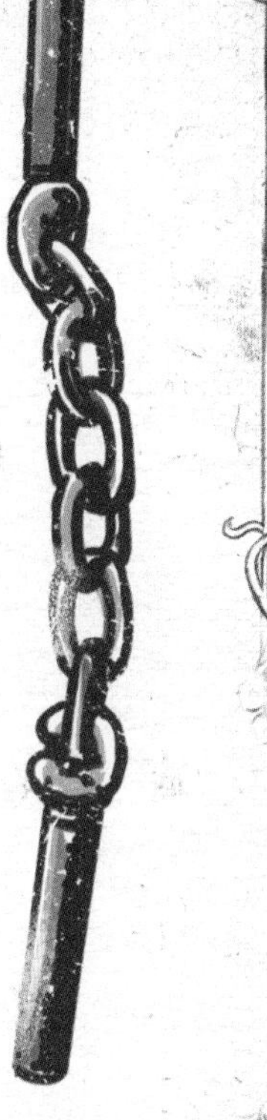

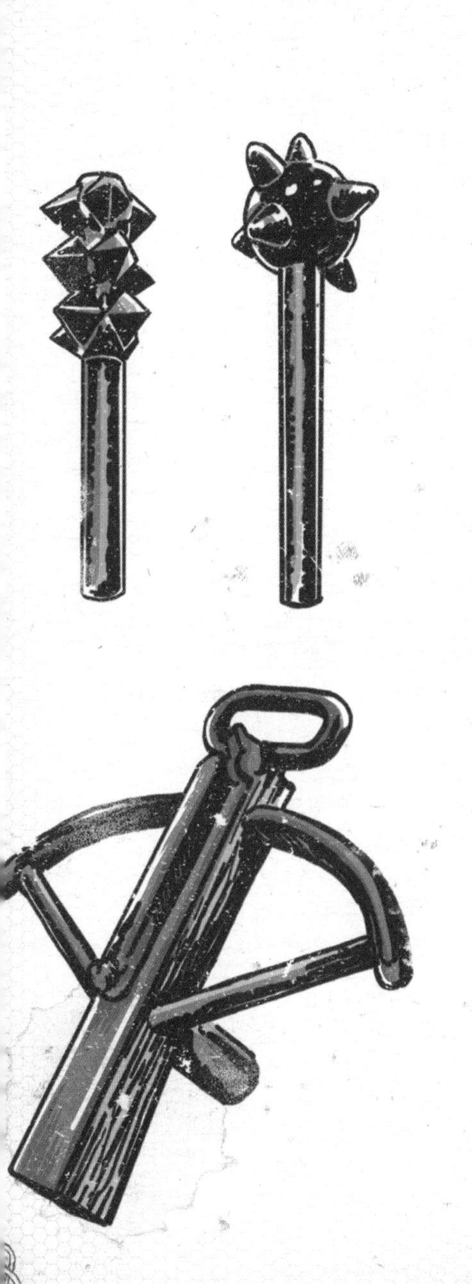

There are many more combat tools available to the aspiring knight. But realistically, they're all useless.

*Hey, I love my axe! :-**

And my lance! :))

And my mace . . . well, at least the modern version of it. :P

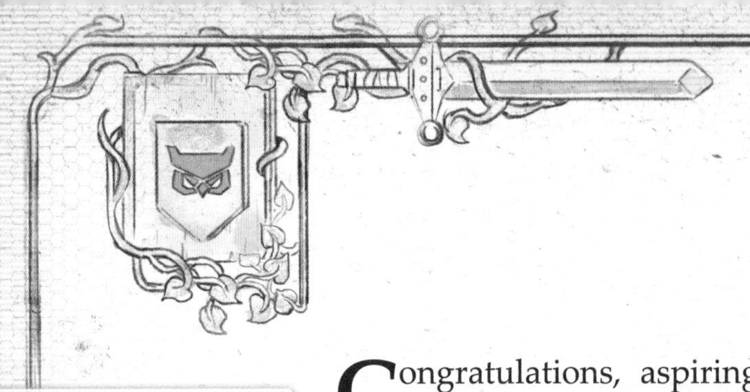

Or . . . you just skipped ahead to the end! That's what I do.

Clay took this part quite literally—he always has this book pretty much glued to his hand. :D

Glad I never had to deal with that guy!

Yeah, but we still had to deal with the other Brickland.

Congratulations, aspiring Knights of the Realm! By making it to the final page of this Knight's Code handbook, you have most likely navigated your first few years of training at the Knights' Academy. By getting this far, you stand a very good chance of living to the ripe old age of fifteen, and even possibly becoming a valuable knight.

All of us at the Knights' Academy and in the kingdom of Knighton are extremely proud of you and wish you much success in your service ahead. Please keep this book close to hand so you can use it to remind yourself of your important duties as a knight. We intend to be constantly updating this volume so it always stays current with all knightly trends.

For the Academy, for the King, and for the Knight's Code . . .

Thunderblood Brickland

THE KNIGHT'S CODE: UPDATE

WRITTEN AND ADDED BY PRINCIPAL BRICKLAND

Aha, here's our Brickland!

And our times!

THE KNIGHTS' ACADEMY CAMPUS

THE KNIGHTS' ACADEMY MOTTO:
"UT AD ARMA, ATQUE AD PROTEGENDUM!"
("Learning to Shield and to Protect!")

The Knights' Academy is located in the heart of the capital city of Knightonia, and has been training knights of the Realm for over 400 years. Now it trains knights who come here to hone their skills, their knowledge, and their chivalry.

THE MAIN BUILDING
Houses the main foyer, cafeteria, auditorium, and most classrooms.

THE GRAND ENTRANCE
Dedicated years ago to King Pike VII.

THE CAFETERIA
Where delicious food is served.

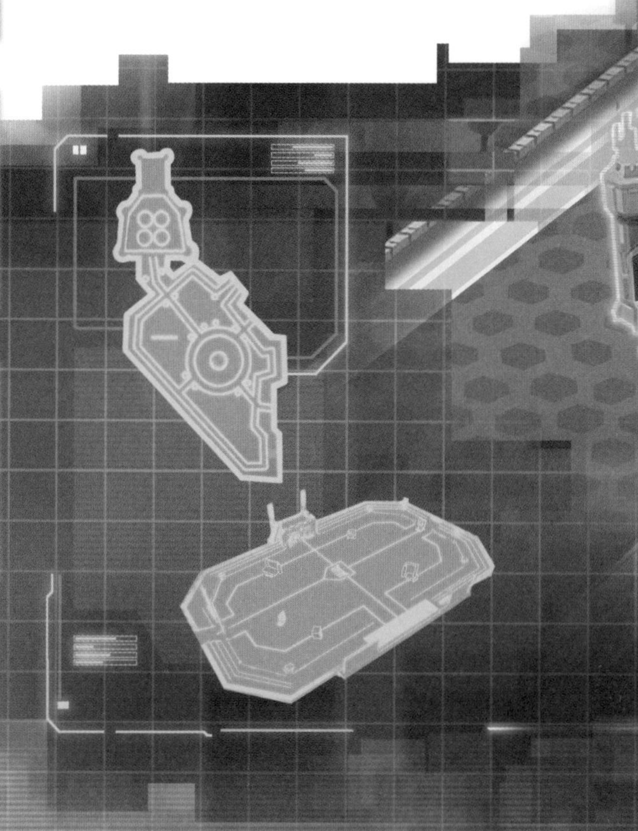

You know what I liked best about the campus? The cafeteria. :)

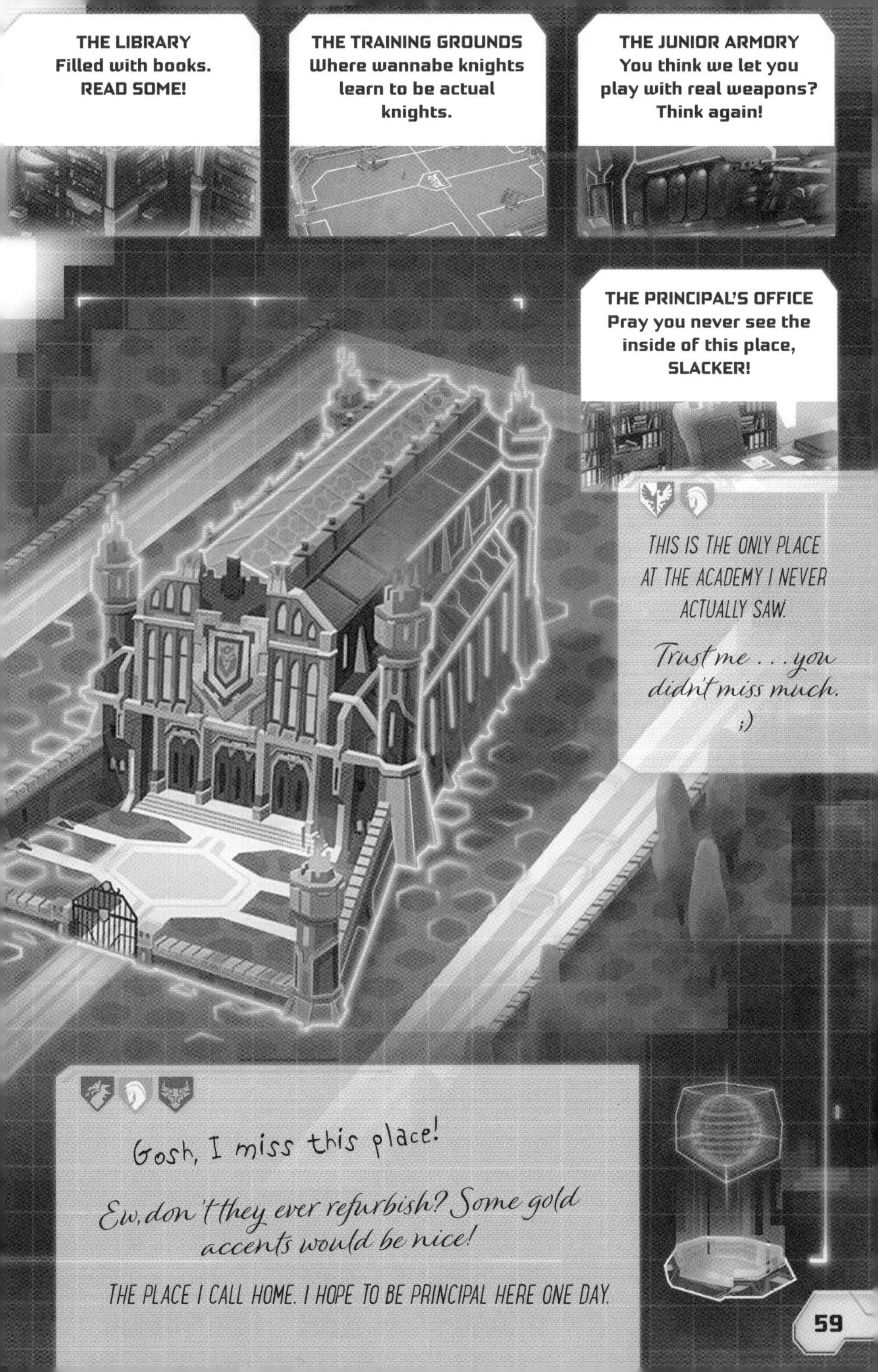
THE LIBRARY
Filled with books. READ SOME!
THE TRAINING GROUNDS
Where wannabe knights learn to be actual knights.
THE JUNIOR ARMORY
You think we let you play with real weapons? Think again!
THE PRINCIPAL'S OFFICE
Pray you never see the inside of this place, SLACKER!
THIS IS THE ONLY PLACE AT THE ACADEMY I NEVER ACTUALLY SAW.
Trust me . . . you didn't miss much. ;)
Gosh, I miss this place!
Ew, don't they ever refurbish? Some gold accents would be nice!
THE PLACE I CALL HOME. I HOPE TO BE PRINCIPAL HERE ONE DAY.

I hate the library. So much reading. I paid someone to read for me.

This was the best place to catch some zzzzs.

THE LIBRARY

The Library is filled with books. Books that will help you learn things and be able to graduate from this glorious institution. The best thing you can do while you're here is stick your nose in a library book and NEVER DO ANYTHING ELSE!

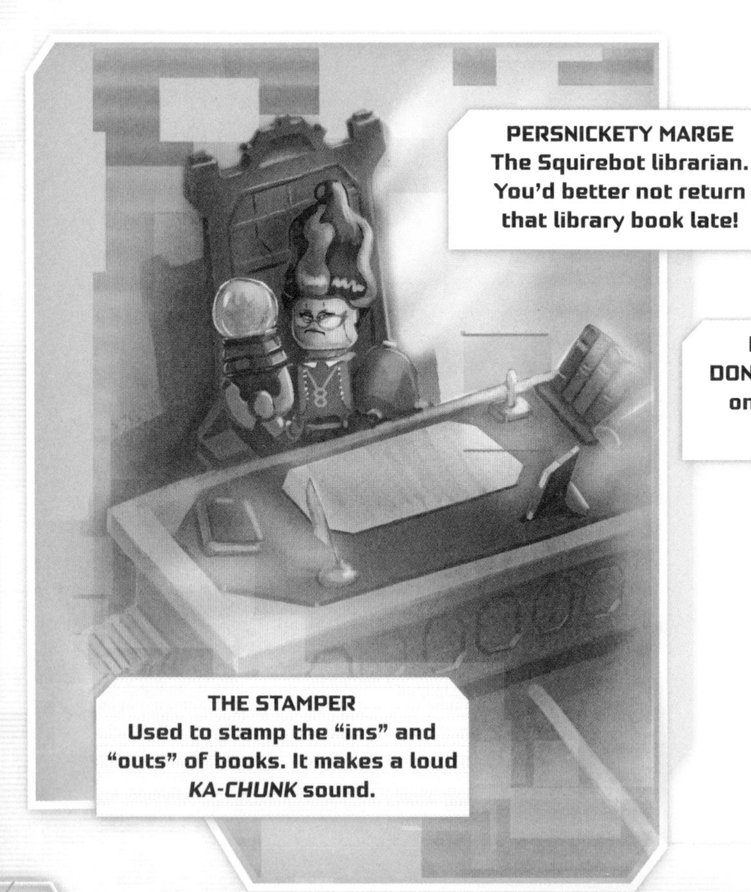

PERSNICKETY MARGE
The Squirebot librarian. You'd better not return that library book late!

MARGE'S DESK
DON'T touch anything on it! (If you value your health!)

THE STAMPER
Used to stamp the "ins" and "outs" of books. It makes a loud *KA-CHUNK* sound.

THE BOOKS ON WEAPONS
Where you should be spending most of your time.
BOOKS
Every library has them.
Thanks, Captain Obvious! :)
BOOK LIFTS
The way you get to books on the higher shelves.
Almost as good as my hover shield. ALMOST. :P
I borrowed every book the library had on Ned Knightly, Knight of Knighton!

I SPENT MOST OF MY SPARE TIME HERE. OK, I SPENT ALL OF MY SPARE TIME HERE.

TRAINING GROUND

A strong body is as important as a strong mind, and knights are made on the training grounds. This is where you practice your teamwork and your moves and become a physically imposing knight of the Realm.

I named my first training lance, Lance. He was my biggest fan.

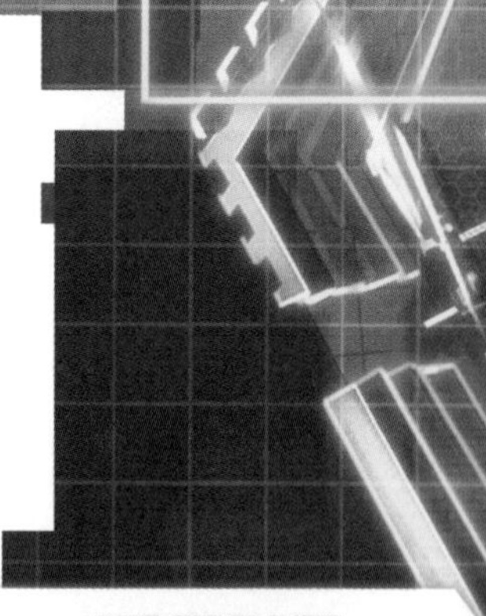

THE ARMS RACK
Pick your best weapon and learn how to use it.

THE SIDELINES
Where you get timed to see just how quickly you can beat the other team.

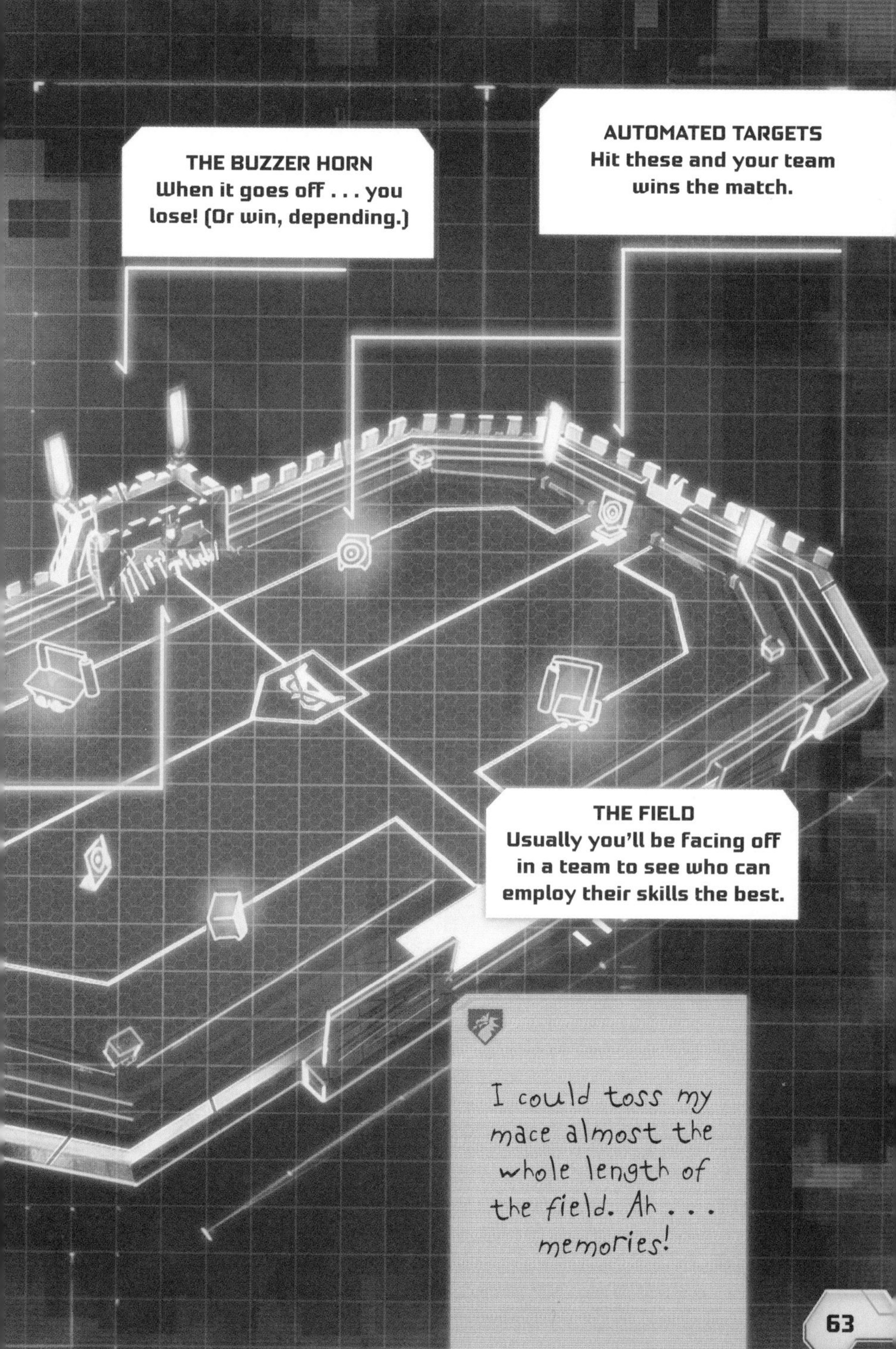
THE BUZZER HORN
When it goes off . . . you lose! (Or win, depending.)
AUTOMATED TARGETS
Hit these and your team wins the match.
THE FIELD
Usually you'll be facing off in a team to see who can employ their skills the best.
I could toss my mace almost the whole length of the field. Ah . . . memories!

I once shot an apple off of some kid's head in this very place. I'm so cool.

CAFETERIA

The cafeteria is where every knight-in-training eats—in an orderly manner—and doesn't spend too much time fooling around. If you want to be really tough, you can order a rock sandwich for lunch. Not good for your teeth, but it makes you really tough.

THE KITCHEN
Famous Chef Gobbleton Rambley created the menu. So if you don't like it, he'll yell at you until you do.

My happiest moments at the Knights' Academy happened here.

THE SERVING LINE
C'mon, keep moving! Everybody needs to eat before lunchtime is over! Stop lollygagging!

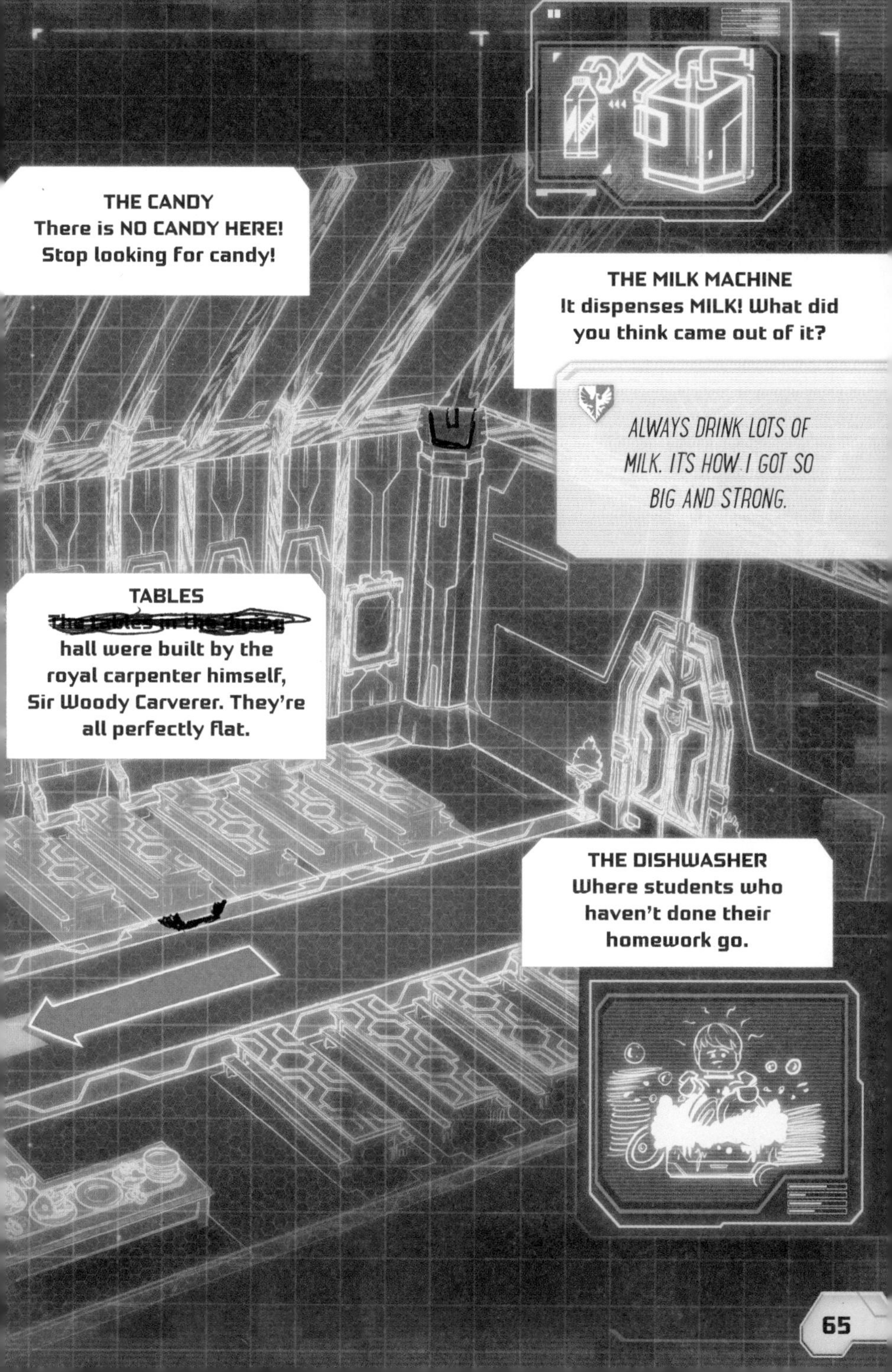
THE CANDY
There is NO CANDY HERE! Stop looking for candy!
THE MILK MACHINE
It dispenses MILK! What did you think came out of it?
ALWAYS DRINK LOTS OF MILK. ITS HOW I GOT SO BIG AND STRONG.
TABLES
hall were built by the royal carpenter himself, Sir Woody Carverer. They're all perfectly flat.
THE DISHWASHER
Where students who haven't done their homework go.

CLASSROOMS

The King Pike IX Learning Center houses most of the Knights' Academy classroom space. It was King Pike IX who first apportioned some gold to build this structure, replacing the academy's original classroom, which consisted of muck-filled tents with dirt floors. (Personally, I think that the students have been too soft ever since.)

THE MERLOK MAGIC LABS
A series of labs where magical experiments and learning can happen in relative safety.

Summonin
a giant
chimera is
always a goo
opportunity
to practice
lab safety
procedures.

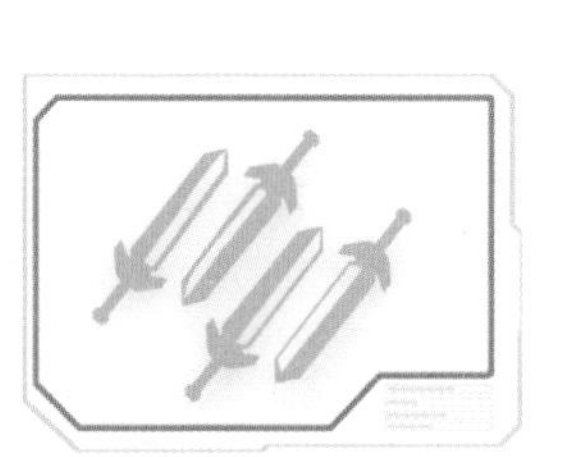

THE SHARPENING ROOM
Learn to be sharper.

THE MATH ROOM
Where your brain goes to experience overheating.

THE JOKES KNIGHTLY LANGUAGE LAB
Sponsored by comedian Jokes Knightly when he was still rich and famous, this is where you can learn to converse with dragons or dwarves.

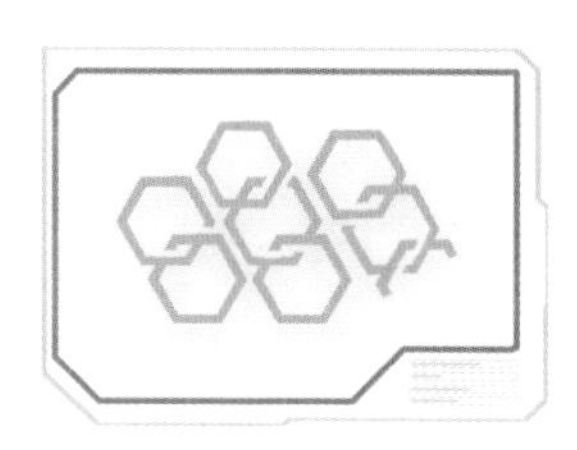

THE CHAIN MAIL ROOM
How to handle your chain mail. There's a test . . . be ready.

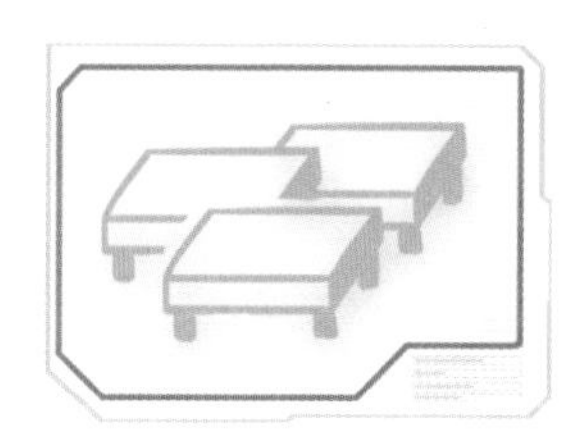

THE CLASSROOM OF CLASSROOMS
Where you learn how to learn. Oh, and you have to do a final project about doing final projects.

THE BRICKNEY SPEARS SPEAR LEARNING ANNEX
In this classroom—sponsored by the famous Knighton pop star—you'll learn everything you ever wanted to know about a spear . . . and more!

THE ART ROOM
Paint your coat of arms—burnt umber is a great base color.

WEAPON MAINTENANCE

The following is a list of Weapon Maintenance Classes that you must take in order to graduate from the Knights' Academy:

A shiny weapon is crucial when you're posing heroically.

Hey Lance, do you use the same wax for polishing your lance as you do for your hair?

I'll have to check with Dennis.

100 LEVEL

- Introduction to Weapon Cleaning: A clean weapon is a happy weapon.
- Introduction to Weapon Maintenance: Maintain it or it will fall apart.
- Polishing Skills for the New Student: Make it shine, people.
- Sheathing: Your weapon should be warm and cosy.

200 LEVEL

- Advanced Weapon Cleaning: Burnishing with a toothbrush.
- Advanced Weapon Maintenance: Take it apart and put it back together while blindfolded.
- Oils, Waxes, Polishes, and Sealers: Know them by smell.
- Introduction to Sharpening: Life's a grind sometimes.

300 LEVEL

- Cleaning Master Class: Blind others with your shiny sword.
- Maintenance Master Class: Take apart a mace and turn it into a sword.
- Advanced Sharpening: Sharp enough to cut rocks in half.
- Arrows for Fun and Profit: Make them, trade them, and shoot 'em into targets!

No way! My mace is aMACYing!

OPEN LEVEL CLASSES

- Pikes and Poleaxes: Keep the bad guys at a distance.
- Shields and Helmets: Stay safe on the battlefield.
- Naming Your Weapons: Treat them like your best friends!
- Magic Weapons: They give you such an edge.

I call mine My Sweet Candy!

I named my lances after the most gallant servants of the Richmond family.

YOU MEAN YOUR NANNIES. RIGHT?

POETRY AND SERENADING

All of the knights
were off fighting dragons.
Except for Lance—
he was at home,
learning how to dance!

Learning to be a well-rounded young knight involves more skills than shining your armor and cleaving things in half. You also need to be chivalrous in your use of . . . words. A top knight should be proficient in poetry and serenading. Here are some examples. (Written by myself, yours truly, of course.)

EXAMPLES OF FINE POETRY:

"Roses are red,
violets are blue,
that puny shield
will not protect you."

"Arrows, arrows, everywhere,
And all the monsters moaned.
Arrows, arrows everywhere . . .
The enemy was *owned.*"

"In Knightonia did King Halbert to
A Knights' Academy decree:
To protect his Realm and lands,
From merciless monster bands,
From the mountains to the sea."

"Roses are red,
violets are blue,
I always eat muffins
and leave none for you!"

All of the knights
went out to see a movie
Except for Clay—
no one told him
it was today!

TIPS FOR SERENADING:

- Learn to play a lute, because if you play a horn you can't sing and play at the same time.
- Warm up your voice before serenading. I do this by randomly yelling at things.
- Pick songs that mention sunsets, love, and flowers, not those that mention monsters, pointy pikes, or magical melty things.
- Always carry flowers without thorns when serenading.
- Make sure you brush your teeth and wax your nose hair before serenading.
- Singing the Knights' Academy School Song is good training for serenading.
- You can often disarm an enemy by suddenly serenading them.

All of the knights were out on a quest, except for Aaron—he was at home, sleeping like a Baron!

ALL OF THE KNIGHTS WERE BATTLING MONSTERS. EXCEPT FOR MACY—SHE WAS AT HOME PLAYING WITH A DOLL NAMED TRACY!

Oh, please, just send them a link to KnighTube.

VEHICLES AND HOW TO DRIVE THEM

An important part of being a modern knight is knowing how to properly handle vehicles of all kinds. Here are some useful tips for driving these vehicles. (Not that I've driven all of them, but I'm the principal here and therefore *always* know best about everything.)

GENERAL VEHICLE DRIVING TIPS:

- Keep your eyes on the road and off the KnightNet while you're driving! (That's an order!)
- Make sure your tires and wheels have no arrows or crossbow bolts stuck in them.
- Wash and wax your vehicle before every battle.
- Clean any and all blasters and pointy bits.
- Keep all lava away from your engine.
- NEVER brake for monsters.
- TURN THAT RADIO DOWN!

Always drive like you're the shiniest, shallowest, most ready-to-fool-around knight there is. I mean, only a Richmond looks good driving a mechanical horse that converts into a motorcycle.

ANY REAL KNIGHT WANTS TO RIDE IN A SWORD-SHAPED VEHICLE. JUST BE CAREFUL NOT TO HIT THE BIG RED BUTTON THAT SHOOTS THE SWORD PART INTO THE AIR LIKE A ROCKET.

Remember this tip: AATTT—Always Accelerate Through The Target! Any monster will be toast. (Or magical fumes as the case may be.)

PHYSICAL EDUCATION

If you can't do 1,000 push-ups in fifteen minutes, you should flunk yourself out of the academy right now! That said, physical education is something that lets you work toward goals, and is one of the most important aspects of being a knight. Hey, if you're not in shape (like me) you can't swing that heavy sword one hundred or so times at that giant monster.

Oh, that's something for Jestro!

SOME OF THE PHYSICAL EDUCATION CLASSES OFFERED AT THE KNIGHTS' ACADEMY:

INTRODUCTION TO RUNNING—Running, followed by some running, with a break for some running.

MACE MASHING 101—Goal: Mace one hundred things with your mace in under ninety seconds.

ARMORED YOGA—You may be in 150 pounds of armor, but you should still be able to wrap your leg around your head. DO IT!

PIKE VAULTING—Can you clear that castle wall? You'd better!

I have everything cleared up by Dennis.

Er, Lance, it is not that kind of clearing they are talking about . . .

THE HAMMER THROW—Queen Halbert still holds the academy's record.

ADVANCED BOW PULLING—Can you fire one hundred arrows in under a minute? You can't? You're worthless and weak.

ADVANCED RUNNING—Running farther, followed by running longer, with tips for running faster (like me following you on a hover horse with a spear!)

MASTER THE AXE—First you start by chopping piles of wood. Then you move on to chopping piles of monsters.

SPEARING—Before you learn to throw a spear, you must learn to *be* a spear. Seriously—stand still while I throw you at the target.

<u>MASTER ADVANCE RUNNING</u>—Just run. Until I tell you to stop. Which will be in about a week from now. RUN!

EXPLORE THE CAMPUS

Many a knight in the kingdom longs for the blissful old days of vigorous study at the academy. But it isn't all studying. Academy life is full of, well . . . life.

Baking Club! Where you learn to make soufflés worthy of knights ;)

But there was never anything left to eat after you joined the club!

EXTRACURRICULAR ACTIVITIES
The great majority of these are not curricular . . . they are extra-curricular. Everything from theater (about knights) to debate clubs (debating knights) and baking club.

THE WISHING WELL
Its cornerstone was laid by King Halbert himself—he loves to toss in a coin and wish someone well.

THE ELECTRIC LUTE ROOM
A good place to cut loose on your electric lute, hyper harp, or harpsichord.

Well, only the extreme nerds can actually master the harpsichord.

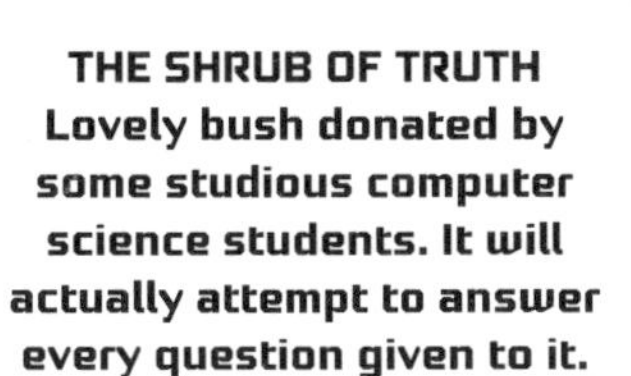

THE SHRUB OF TRUTH
Lovely bush donated by some studious computer science students. It will actually attempt to answer every question given to it.

CHIVALROUS ROOM
There are many spots on campus to let your mind wander to chivalrous thoughts: the gardens, the library . . . the CHIVALROUS ROOM where you can practice chivalrousness with a Squirebot trained by Haute Fancypants, the King's own servant.

Shouldn't it be a damsel instead of a bot?

No damsel could bear your attempts at chivalry! :)

THE ATTIC OF STUFF
Many a student will do their voluntary clean-up duty in the attic of the academy, simply to see all the wondrous things there including: Ned Knightly's toenail clippings (not authenticated) and Sir Griffiths' stuffed pet griffin, who he named Griff.

THE PATH OF ENLIGHTENMENT
Stepping stones in the garden that lay out some good tips for leading a knightly life. Tip number one: Pretend that everywhere except for these stepping stones is lava . . . now . . . don't fall into the lava!

THE POLISH PARLOR
Have some extra coinage? Get the Squirebots in this space to do all your polishing for you.

FESTIVALS AND COMPETITIONS

The Knights' Academy trains students to be the ultimate competitors. Naturally, festivals and competitions (and festivals *about* competitions) are a vital part of academy life.

THE PRINCIPAL'S TOURNAMENT
The end of the academic year festival that lets students of every level show off their skills. Everyone wants to win Brickland's Brick—the tournament's ultimate trophy.

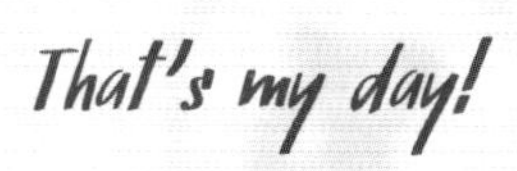

BOWDACIOUS DAY
A chance to show what can be done with a bow or crossbow. Shoot targets, split apples on friends' heads, play your bow like a guitar . . . it's all part of Bowdacious Day!

And that's MY day. What armor is best? The shiny stuff!

ARMOR DAY
Students get a chance to show off their best armors.

SPRING JOUST
Grab a hover horse, a lance, and a quality helmet, and get out and see who can knock the other one off!

FALL THEATER FEST
Enjoy classic plays by Quakespear, the most famous ancient playwright in Knighton. This year saw a production of his most classic play, *Hammerlet*.

My favorite is Titus Brickonicus.

I could easily play in both.

THE ALUMNI TOURNAMENT
A chance for the students to battle some famous alumni.

You'll let Brickland win if you know what's good for you.

THE SINGING SWORD SONG COMPETITION
A chance to have your name engraved on the Singing Sword for the boomiest voice of any academy student.

THE QUEEN OF CLEAN FESTIVAL
Grab a hammer and reshingle the roof to the Grand Hall! This festival was founded by Queen Halbert who loves to hammer.

THE "DANCE 'TIL YOU DROP" WINTER FORMAL
Put on your best clothes, and you and your date must try to be the last couple dancing to win this prom/competition combination.

THE CURRENT RECORD IS ELEVEN DAYS.

And it belongs to my mom. Again.

CHIVALRY DEBATE TOURNAMENT
Placing your cloak over a puddle or using your helmet to boil soup for starving orphans—which is more chivalrous? Argue it out at the tournament!

INTEREST GROUPS

What clubs and groups might there be at the Knights' Academy? Glad you asked! There are many different interest groups that are officially sanctioned:

Poleaxes are good for scratching your back with! :)

KNIGHT CLUB
Earn your merit badges for knightly activities like: chain mail repair, wound lancing, digital fire building, and finding alternate uses for an axe.

I was there!

THE KINGSMEN
The official academy Glee Club that sings updated arrangements of old classics like "Cut Out that Dragon's Tongue" (the mech-hop update), "Boiled in Oil, Oil, Oil!," and "The Sword Swingers Theme in C-Sharp."

Gotta collect them all.

Yeah, you attended each club. Just once.

CLUB CLUB
Collect, trade, and use your favorite clubs with your academy peers.

SWIM CLUB
Can you actually swim in armor? You're going to find out.

ARCHERS ANONYMOUS
For the kids who just gotta shoot, shoot, shoot arrows.

SHIELDS AND SPEARS
The club for students in
the upper ten percent of their class.

I FELT PRETTY LONELY IN THIS CLUB.

STUDY OR GET EXPELLED
The club for students in
the lower ten percent of their class.

I didn't feel lonely here. It's an elite club. Deal with it.

HELMET HAIR
Grooming tips for everyone who wears armor.

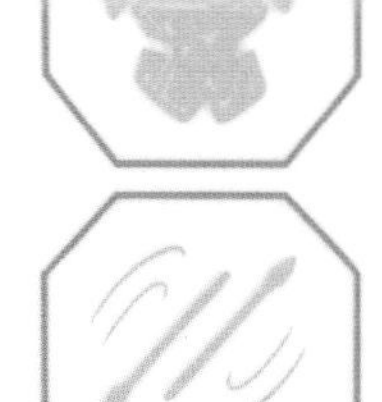

SYNCHRONIZED SPEARING
Can you dance and hurl a spear at the same time? I bet you can!

DUNGEON DIVERS' CLUB
Wanna explore every dark, musty dungeon in the kingdom? You can do it with the special field trips sponsored by this club.

LIVING CHESS CLUB
Compete with actual people as the pieces—bishops, rooks, knights, etc. Fun for all ages.

Didn't like it.

Maybe you didn't like it because you can't actually play chess? :)

MAGIC DEBATE SOCIETY
Use your magic powers to make a point . . . or to clamp a magic mouth-plug onto your opponent's yapper.

MECH CLUB
Gearheads and Mech Makers build and battle with their favorite mechs.

THE SQUIREBOTS

While the squire has enjoyed being a long and noble tradition in Knighton, this role has undergone a dramatic change due to technological innovations. The kingdom's inventors have elaborated a highly efficient service android known as the Squirebot—designed to automate all tasks currently performed by human squires. Squirebots assist our knights, as well as handling every menial task around. The new Squirebots are the epitome of physical and mechanical perfection, flawlessly executing their duties and protecting the kingdom from threats. I have asked our academy experts to compile a list of dos and don'ts for students to consider when dealing with androids.

They're great at holding up targets and running away screaming!

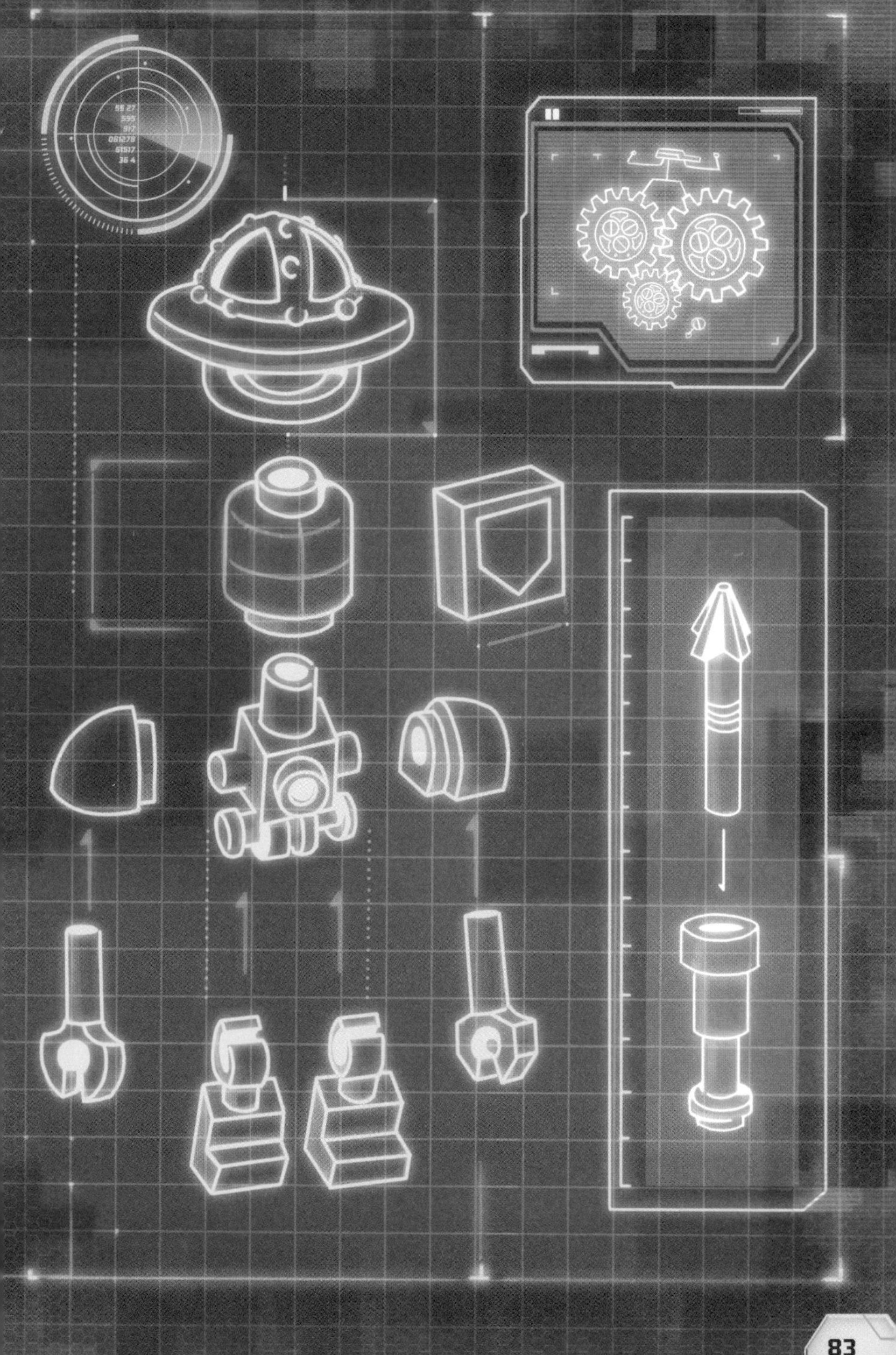
55 27
595
917
061278
51517
36 4

So they can mess them up—I'm talking about you, butterbot Dennis

Any chore is a challenge.

I once met a Squirebot with a pet toaster. He named him Gutsy.

How adorable! ;)

How tragic! What a waste of a good toaster. :P

SQUIREBOT DOS AND DON'TS

. . . DO
assign them all your most challenging chores.

. . . DO
keep them properly charged and maintained.

. . . DO
give them a compliment every so often—Squirebots have "feelings," too.

. . . DON'T
feed them sticky food, or any food for that matter. They're machines. They don't need nutrition.

Oh, now I know why Axl is always cooking with Chef Eclair.

Our comradery runs deep.

As deep as your stomach, no doubt!

. . . DON'T
hit them with heavy objects, vehicles, or explosives.

. . . DON'T
laugh at them should they ever get comically hurt in the execution of their duties. Which is often.

Oops. :)

TOP BOTS OF KNIGHTON

#1 ALICE SQUIRES

Knighton's most popular, on-air Holovision personality. "Queen of Happy Talk" Alice, works on KNN and hosts infotainment spectacu-galas, as well as working the red carpet at Holo-Wood premieres with her CamBot, Riccardo. Alice's specialties include celebrity gossip, staring dreamily at famous actors, and being FABULOUS!

#2 HAUTE FANCYPANTS

The King's rather proper right-hand bot, Haute FancyPants, pretty much runs the kingdom. He ensures the castle lights stay on, the hover-trains run, and the King does not destroy himself doing whatever it is he does all day. FancyPants believes the earth is shaped like a giant banana and is allergic to velvet rope.

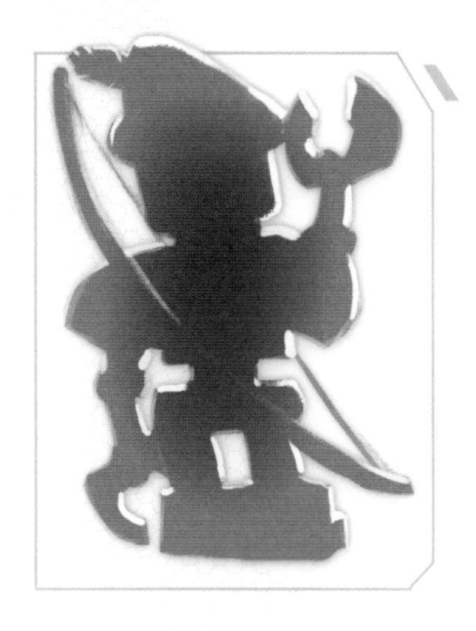

#3 ROBOT HOODLUM
Rumors abound about a once-faithful Squirebot who has gone rogue and now hides out in a petrified forest on the edge of Knighton with his gang of "Merry Mechs." Legend has it that this outlaw bot robs from the rich so that he may help the poor and broken Squirebots of the kingdom. But most people believe the "Robot Hoodlum" is just a robot fairy tale.

#4 CHEF ÉCLAIR
One of the kingdom's greatest culinary masters, Chef Éclair speaks with a French accent. Why does a robot have a French accent? Who knows? Perhaps he learned it while studying at Knighton's Culinary Academy with super-famous chef Gobbleton Rambley. Whatever his language is, there's only one word you need to know when he's around—YUM!

I REMEMBER JESTRO BREAKING A SERVANTBOT.

Was his joke that bad?

IT WAS A RIDDLE. IT STARTED WITH, "I ONLY LIE. I'VE NEVER, EVER SAID ANYTHING TRUE."

But if what he said was true, that meant he wasn't lying.

It must have caused a loop in the bot's brain.

Mine as well. Thinking makes me hungry. :/

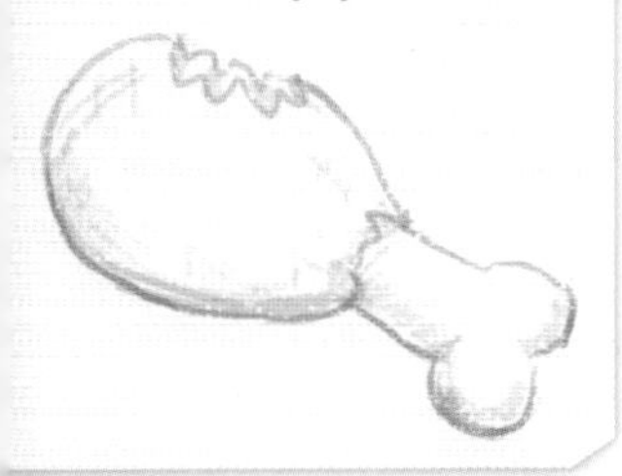

MISCELLANEOUS BOTS

These are not famous individuals, but they are some of the kingdom's most popular types of Squirebots.

SERVANTBOTS

Let's give a big cheer for the good old basic servantbots. They are assigned to do anything requested of them by a master. At the academy, most of their tasks involve setting up absurdly dangerous stunts and then jumping frantically out of the way.

GUARDBOTS

Who protects our kingdom? Guardbots, that's who. The truth is, their battle skills are extremely limited. However, they are proficient at getting randomly smashed by monsters and/or running away screaming.

FARMERBOTS

Okay, robots don't even eat food, so why do they run all the farms in the kingdom? Because no one else wants to! Plus, they not only plant and pick all the crops, but they also make excellent scarecrows. Just make sure the sprinklers aren't on when they're out in the fields or they'll rust in place.

HERALDBOTS

Knighton may be one of the most digital kingdoms around, but some things still need to be delivered by hand—robot hand, that is. Heraldbots race around as fast as their little legs will carry them with head-sirens blaring to deliver news, packages, and even takeout food.

Can't fight on an empty stomach!

ACTORBOT

Yikes! Is that a Scurrier? No, it's just a Squirebot in costume. So convincing! This is the actorbot class of droid—normal Squirebots who perform in Knighton video and theater productions. They have a surprising dramatic range and big screen presence.

They do all their own stunts! Tell them to break a leg and they will! SNAP!

ENTERTAINERBOT

Much like an actorbot, this Squirebot's duty is to perform for audiences across the Realm. They sing, they dance, they tell jokes. Enjoy at your own risk.

I never actually liked how they performed. Too stiff. Too . . . machine-like.

KING EGGRED HALBERT

His Majesty, King Halbert, is one of the Knights' Academy's most famous students. His father, King Thinneous "The Nervous" Halbert II, worried about his son's future (he worried about almost everything). But after King Halbert attended the academy, the world was his oyster—his end-of-term project was about ancient mapmakers who used molluscs as navigational aids. Though he proved himself as a knight, it was really his benevolence that got him recognized. He was always very thoughtful and good, and tried to make everything around him just and fair. (In fact, he organized the first "Just and Fair Fair" while he was a student.)

I HOPE YOU KNELT BEFORE READING THIS PASSAGE—IT SHOWS PROPER RESPECT TO HIS HIGHNESS.

Do you kneel every time you read about the King in the papers, too?

That would make reading a newspaper on the toilet pretty tough.

QUEEN HAMA HALBERT

Her Majesty, Queen Hama Halbert, entered the academy as a commoner. She quickly earned her title—"The Kicker of Butts"—for her hard work on the training ground with her favored weapon, the hammer. Boy could she kick butt. She was the first freshman student to be President of the Impact Instrument Club, and she was the lead striker for the Brickland Brick-winning tournament teams, in year 004, 005, and 006. She was also in the glee club and every tapestry-dying tournament in her senior year.

One day I hope to become royal.

That's not really how it works, Lance.

SIR SWORDMORE BRICKLAND

Sir Brickland is not only this school's principal and the editor of this handbook; he is also the single most important figure in the history of this academy! (Editor's note: this is a completely true fact; no exaggeration.) The mighty Brickland began his career as a heroic, monster-fighting warrior, teaming with (future) King Halbert and (overrated) superstar Ned Knightly. Brickland's undeniable leadership skills led to an appointment as principal of the academy during what he calls, "The Golden Age of Knight Schooling." With the kingdom free of monsters and most major threats, the academy became a lightly-attended and easily-managed institution of relaxing—er, learning. For several decades, the academy only graduated a few students a year, allowing Brickland plenty of free time to work on his second career as a minstrel playwright.

Hey!
Ned Knightly was definitely NOT overrated. He was the coolest Knightonian ever and a total legend.

Sorry, Macy. That title has now been taken (hint: by me).

YOU played HIM in a film, not the other way around. Your opinion is invalid.

Ha! So you did watch it! :P

NED KNIGHTLY

One of the most famous knights to ever graduate from the Knights' Academy, Knightly went on to star in several bestselling comic books, feature films, and 5D holographic epics. But as Principal Brickland (editor of this handbook) explains: "I went to school with Ned Knightly and Ned Knightly . . . was no Ned Knightly." In other words, the real Ned fell a few gauntlets short of his full-fisted legend. This "hero of heroes" really just had a good publicist. He spent a lot more time at school gardening and practicing his Dutch Clogging skills than honing his warrior abilities. In fact, during The Great Battle at the Golden Castle, Ned was in the latrine, leaving the REAL heroics to the Mighty Brickland. (Editor's note: still not exaggerating.) Ned's brother, Jokes Knightly, is far more noble and entertaining.

Hey, how come none of us are on this list?

Famous? None of these people are as famous as I am!

A TRUE KNIGHT DOESNT WANT TO BE FAMOUS. A TRUE KNIGHT WANTS TO SEEK JUSTICE IN OBSCURITY.

Such a notion sounds obscure to me!

OTHER FAMOUS ALUMNI

Over the years, the Knights' Academy has had many, many famous graduates. (In some cases, when we say, "famous" we mean, "infamous.") Here is a sampling of some of them:

JORAH TIGHTWAD—One of the richest, fattest, and most egomaniacal men in the kingdom, "The One Who Doesn't Spend a Penny" became famous for finishing leftover food from other students' plates.

SIR GRIFFITHS—His best friend at the academy is now the principal (Brickland). Though he went on to become a famously brave and honorable knight, while at the academy, he and "Binky" Brickland accumulated more demerits than any other students.

JURGEN VON STROHEIM—Now a famous film director, Jurgen Von Stroheim began his career as a knight and graduate of the academy. But he was better with a camera than he was with a sword and became much more deadly in the editing room than on the training grounds.

JOKES KNIGHTLY—With a disarming sense of humor, many thought Jokes made the academy a more fun place. Others thought his dumb puns and stupid knock-knock jokes made life at the academy intolerable. He decided he liked making laughs more than making chivalry, so he became a comedian.

BRICKNEY SPEARS—Famous for her singing and spear work at the academy, Brickney Spears went on to become a well-known pop star in Knighton. Her moves with a spear are great . . . but only in rehearsal. In real combat, she's in trouble.

CONCLUSIONS

End of the beginning? What of the what? Brickland's like the riddle-master!

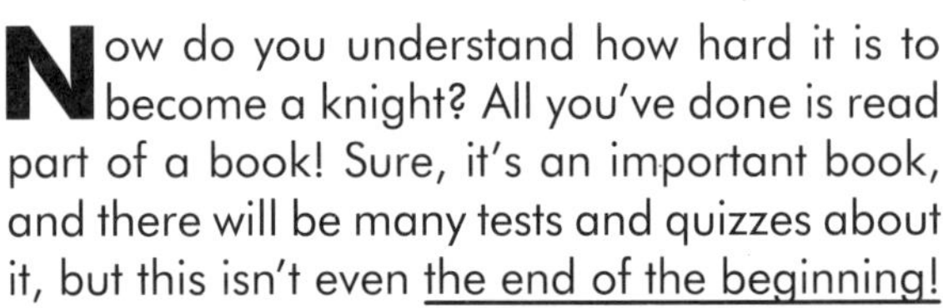

Now do you understand how hard it is to become a knight? All you've done is read part of a book! Sure, it's an important book, and there will be many tests and quizzes about it, but this isn't even the end of the beginning!

What do you do now? Find a grindstone and put your nose on it. All night if you have to, and all day as well. The best advice I can give you right now is summed up in one word: WORK. HARD. Okay, so that's two words, but stop editing the editor and WORK HARD. You understand me, squire? Read over this section again. I sense a surprise test coming tomorrow . . .

Your hardworking principal setting a shining example,

Sir Swordmore Brickland

TESTS ARE IMPORTANT. THEY KEEP YOU SHARP. LIKE A SWORD. ONLY FOR YOUR BRAIN. I LIKE HAVING A SHARP SWORD-BRAIN.

Read, read, read. There are sooo many better ways to spend your time. I always paid people to read for me.

THE KNIGHT'S CODE: DIGITAL EDITION

WHEN POWERS GET DIGITAL

BY MERLOK 2.0

Merlok 2.0 here to, um, err . . . to talk about what us digital wizards (well that's just me, really) like to refer to as the "digital age" of knighthood. It appears that monsters have returned to Knighton, so the time has come for us to use more than the usual swords and shields to protect our kingdom—the time has come for us to use . . . NEXO Powers. Oh my, that sounded so dramatic.

What are NEXO Powers, you ask? Well, er, let me start by revealing some of the secrets to my high-tech amazingness . . .

Yoo-hoo!

It's not that much of a mystery!—Ava

<u>NEXO Powers allow me to download all sorts of incredible powers that are stored in my digital, magical memory.</u> Right yes, okay, I know you're waiting for me to say something wise and mage-like. So, here goes: Young knights-in-training, learn everything you can about how to use your NEXO Powers. It will serve you well in defending the Kingdom of Knighton.

Now, I shall try to go into a bit more detail . . .

And so will the great vehicles that I made.
—Robin

Congrats on your first digi sticky note, Robin!

I used to just like bashing stuff, but NEXO Powers are very cool. I can't really function without them now.

NEXO POWERS ARE COOL INDEED. BUT WE NEED TO MAKE SURE WE REMEMBER THE LESSONS OF THE PAST AND MIX THEM WITH THE TECHNOLOGY OF THE FUTURE.

Oh, barf! Why do you always have to be the "uptight knight?" "Embrace the future," I say.

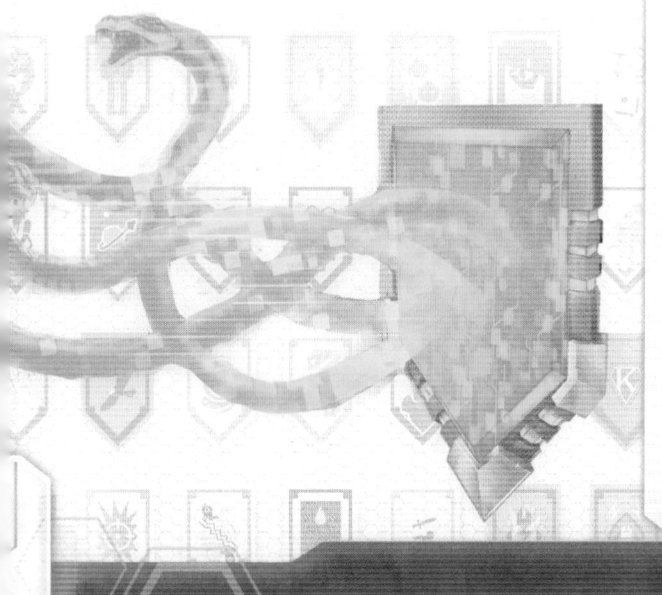

NEXO POWERS

BY MERLOK 2.0

It has to be said that the single greatest advancement in the conduct and performance of a knight's duty has been the introduction of NEXO Powers.

NEXO Powers are a type of um . . . er . . . magical enhancement to a knight's combat skills. In the past, such powers were provided by potions, spells, and talismans . . . oh, those were such magical times . . . but I digress, so let me get back to the point . . . these new upgrades can now be wirelessly downloaded in a digital form.

You can receive these digital downloads to your shields or other gear. Receiving one will provide you with a variety of extraordinary powers like the Anvil of Trouble, Banana Bombs, Bubble Gum Misfire (my personal favorite), Chicken Power, Funky Fungus, and many, many more. Downloads are essential for battling the many new and exceptionally powerful monsters that have afflicted the kingdom as of late. But to be honest, most people don't actually understand how NEXO Powers work.

To help explain this further, I have turned to one of the kingdom's main experts in this discipline, who also just happens to be our technological wunderkind here on the Fortrex . . . Ava Prentis.

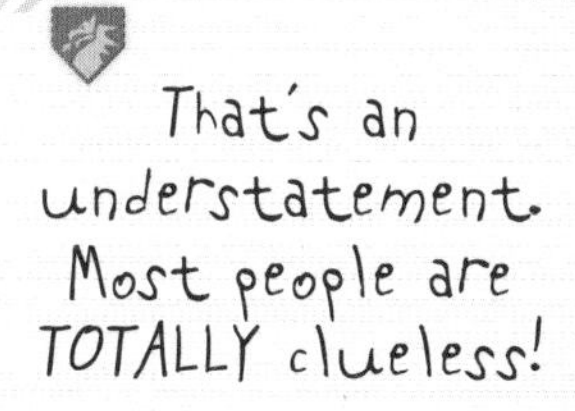

Woo-hoo! Go Ava!

*You got this one.
Show 'em how it's
done!*

Uh . . .
Sorry, Ava, I'm not sure what to write.

Yeah, now that you WANT us to make fun of your page, it's not really much . . . fun . . . anymore.

HOW NEXO POWERS WORK

EXPLAINED BY AVA PRENTIS

So I know that everyone who has one of these books pastes digital sticky notes all over it. So I'm just going to give you a little space to get that out of your system. Here goes . . .

You go, girl! You totally shut down those doodling doofuses!

CARRY ON, AVA. YOU ARE WISE BEYOND YOUR YEARS.

Uh, can I still draw a mustache on her picture?

Now that you've had your creative freedom, I think we can get down to business (nice mustache by the way—I assume you've marked up my picture as well). Anyway . . . the concept behind NEXO Powers is simple enough to understand. But first, you have to understand a little bit about the nature of magic. To be blunt, there's no great "magic" about magic. It is simply the expression of language, gestures, and symbols in order to call forth a supernatural force. This language often takes the form of spells. And spells are just another form of data—information that can be processed by a machine. Once this data is entered into a computer system, it can be processed, modified, and then output to an end user. You, the knight, are the end user.

It's kind of like sending a picture of a flower from your computer to your printer. The power and beauty of the flower remains intact regardless of what form it takes, whether it's lighting up your screen or hanging on your wall as a piece of paper. It's the same with spells and magic.

Whoaa . . . She's makin' my head spin.

PAY ATTENTION. YOU'LL LEARN SOMETHING.

Maybe . . .

I get hungry when I'm confused. Cupcakes! Yum!

And cupcakes!

But like any kind of technological advancement, there are glitches and quirks in both the input and output systems. For starters, one has to get the initial "magic" data into the system. It's possible to type or scan some forms of magic into a modern NEXO KNIGHTS hero's system, but the way our system got its initial input was the result of a fierce, old-fashioned magical battle between Merlok and the powerful Book of Monsters in Merlok's Library at the King's castle. The conflict ended in a massive, magical explosion that destroyed most of the library, and inadvertently sent Merlok, and all of his magical energy, into the castle's computer system.

Another way of putting it: This magical explosion was the most significant "Act of Data Entry" that the world has ever known. The castle's computer now contained all the spells and energy of the most powerful wizard in the kingdom. With a few tweaks here and there, our team was able to restore and process this magical energy into the NEXO Powers now used by the Knights.

Again with the understatement.

Yes! I see the word "battle." Now that I understand.

I love how Ava makes something like "data entry" sound exciting.

I'm just giving you a simple technical explanation. Merlok is now literally inside the computers we use on our rolling castle—the Fortrex. He exists in a digital form we call Merlok 2.0. He helps run our castle and our gear, as well as distributes his powerful digital magic when needed. It is not a perfect system. We may be dealing with a type of magic here, but that doesn't mean its processing and delivery is always magical.

For now, just be aware that digital magic is here to help you and your kingdom. Study this book and practice its recommendations, and you, too, will one day be a great NEXO KNIGHTS hero. Or, if you're really smart, you can come work in the Fortrex Command Center with me. And I'll show you something REALLY exciting—lines and lines of computer code!

Did she just use the word "simple"?

I think I need another cupcake.

Chasing monsters; boooring, Riding a hover shield; exciting, watching lines of computer code; REALLY exciting ;P Go AVA!

SHIELDS

EXPLAINED BY AVA PRENTIS

I also use mine For Flying! Woo-hoo!

A shield is possibly the most important component employed by a NEXO KNIGHTS hero in his or her battle against evil. This ability to receive downloads is what distinguishes a shield from all other handheld protective armaments. Its unique metals and embedded receptor strips enable it to attract and process the powerful digi-magic downloads. The shield then disburses this power to the rest of the armor and weapons used by the knight.

My shield makes me look really cool! The light bounces off of it to perfectly light up my strong, leading-man features.

UGHHH . . . GIVE ME A BREAK. IT'S NOT A BEAUTY PRODUCT. IT'S FOR COMBAT!

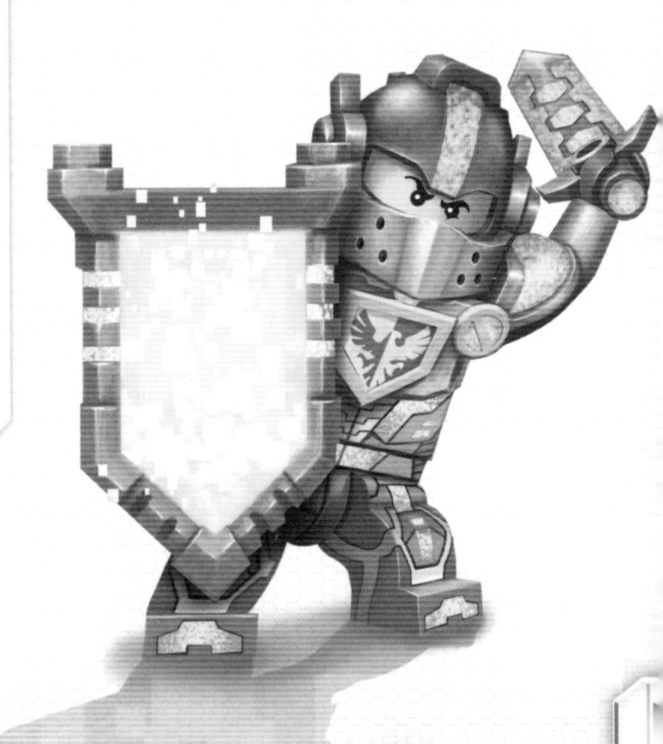

Students at the academy will be provided with what is known as the Student Shield— a slightly smaller version of the traditional shield. Once a student's training is complete at the academy, he or she will receive an official Knight's Shield of the Realm at their graduation ceremony. Thus, they become SHIELD BEARERS.

Below is a sample of some existing NEXO KNIGHTS shields.

Logging off,
Ava Prentis
Knights' Academy Apprentice

"Student Shield"? More like "Baby Shield."

Unless your dad (the King) won't let you have one.

Sorry about getting cupcake icing everywhere!

CLAY'S SHIELD

NOTE THE NOBLE FALCON ON MY SHIELD. IT STANDS FOR HONOR, JUSTICE, AND COURAGE.

Or . . . maybe it just means you're a birdbrain! Ha, ha, ha, ha!

LANCE'S SHIELD

My shield has the mighty horse. It represents all that is me—strong, handsome, and ready to race.

UGH . . .
I THINK IT JUST MEANS YOURE A BEAST OF BURDEN . . . TO ME!

AARON'S SHIELD

Check out the fox, dudes! Just like my last name—Aaron Fox! Oh, and I rigged my shield so it can fly and hover. Why? Because it's AWESOME!

MACY'S SHIELD

It took a while, but I finally got my mother's old shield—Dragon Fire. And, yes, it's a little pink. But if you EVER make fun of it, you'll feel its burn!

I THINK YOUR SHIELD'S AMAZING, MACY. AND WELL-DESERVED.

Oh, you're such a suck-up, birdbrain.

AXL'S SHIELD

My shield has a bull on it. Most people think this represents strength. I think it represents . . . beef products!

Yum!

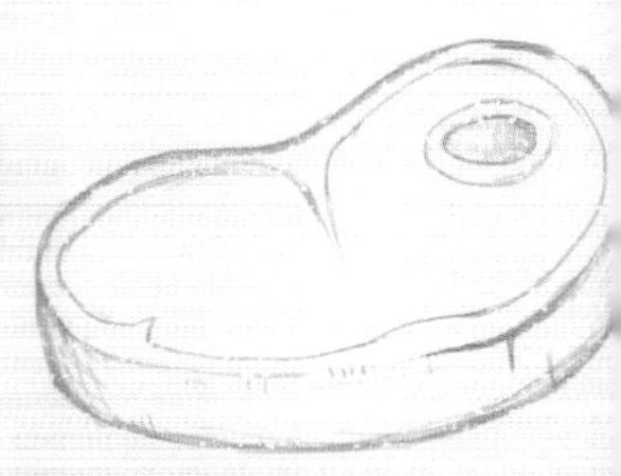

THE BEST POWERS

BY MERLOK 2.0

So, now you know how it all really works. I expect Ava would have probably explained it better, but anyway . . . It is time to present the best of the best powers. NEXOOOO KNIGHTS!

Indeed ;)

Well, maybe a little.

This reminds me of something . . . that's it! It smells like Whiparella's Toxic Perfume!

Peweeeew!

Sour strike—You leave a poisonous trail behind you.

Fist Smash—Five giant fists come down from the sky one after the other, and pound enemies.

THIS IS MY FAVORITE. NEXT TO GLORY OF KNIGHTON AND THE CHAMPION OF CHIVALRY.

Power of United Knights—Call out for one of your fellow knights to help you in battle.

Magnetize—A mystic energy that violently pulls all enemies together.

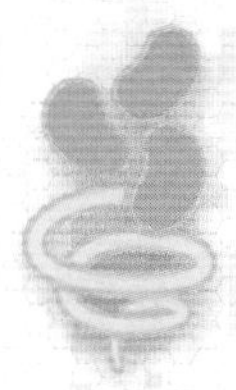

Bonkers Beans—Turn your enemies crazy with these barmy jelly beans.

Draining scarf—You entangle enemies with scarves and mummify them.

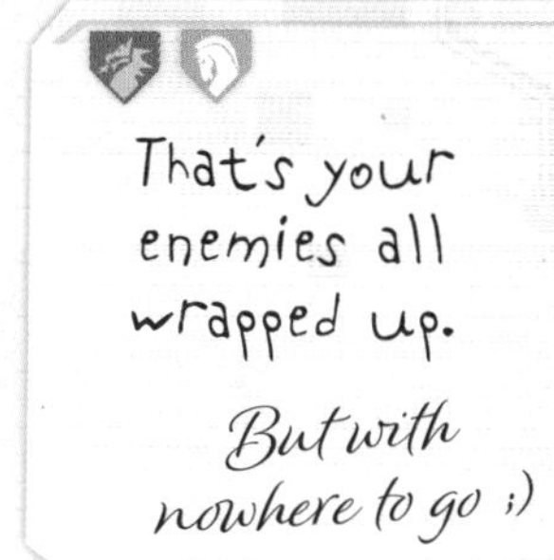

Chicken Power—Smash and distract your enemies with eggs falling from the sky.

Rock and Roll—Hear a guitar rift with every strike.

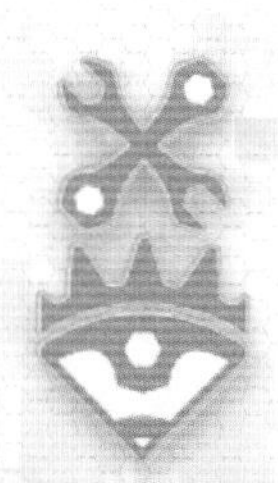

Mech Master—The knight summons his or her Squirebot to help him or her in battle.

Bubble Gum Misfire —You create a bubblegum sphere around yourself.

I'd like a strawberry flavored one, please.

HQ AND VEHICLES

BY ROBIN UNDERWOOD

I do enjoy some quality time in the lounge the most.

You're not supposed to be lounging all the time, Lance.

I would have said it was super, super cool. I like the word cool. And super.

IT MEETS MY HIGH STANDARDS FOR A BATTLE TRAINING FACILITY.

Oh, I think I've left a soufflé in the oven.

So what's the problem with a castle? It just sits there waiting to be attacked, that's what. But the Fortrex? Well, it's a completely cool, powered rolling fortress. It's got everything a NEXO KNIGHTS hero needs: a place to sleep, a command center, a garage, an armory, a holo training room, a kitchen, and a lounge. All this and big tank treads, too. Like, really big. Bet you wish you had one, huh?

THE FORTREX

EXTERIOR VIEW

Power Lines—Running throughout the Fortrex

The Parapet—Where you can look out over the countryside, or where you can fire at monsters

I thought it was just for firing at monsters.

I thought it was just for looking out over the countryside. :)

Hologram Banners—These can display almost anything and are holographic

We should display some of my selfies in our next battle!

The Bowtrex—A big crossbow atop the Fortrex that can launch all sorts of things (including Squirebots)

Defense Towers—For "towering" over monsters and dropping stuff on their heads

View Screen Shield—On the front of the Fortrex so folks inside can talk to people outside

Blasters—For blasting back bad guys at close range

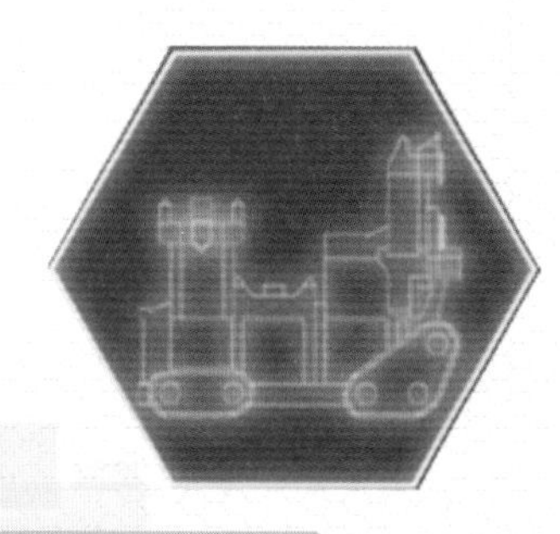

Drawbridge Door—The main door of the Fortrex (It helps with getting in and getting out.)

THE FORTREX

IN ACTION!

The blasters fire automatically if bad guys get too close.

WHAM!
Ol' Burnzie gets "draw-bridged"! Eas
pickings for Axl.

Look, it's me! Sending some Squirebots into battle! That Bowtrex is fun and battle-ready.
ROBIN. YOUR STRATEGIC PLANNING SKILLS ARE A REAL VIRTUE.
But he is quite literally, sending Squirebots flying into battle . . .

Chef Éclair gets in on the action . . . in the most delicious way.
It's a long (and delicious) way down to the pit of my stomach. :D

COMMAND CENTER

THIS IS WHERE IT ALL HAPPENS AND WHERE THE GANG HANGS OUT, CRUSHING DIGITS AND THE LIKE.

Great use of the word "crushing," Robin. I LOVE crushin' everything!

My workstation is very utilitarian. Because it's a workstation.

Side note: Merlok 2.0 can download almost any song you could ever want.
Never thought my dad's motorized caravan would be completely computerized. He's not so into the high-tech stuff.
This place is like something out of a cheesy sci-fi Holovision show. I would have used more gold in its design.

KNIGHTS' QUARTERS

EVERYONE NEEDS SOME ZZZZ TIME.

Is this room empty? Oh no, wait–it's just Clay's room :P

Hey, Clay! You should tidy up!

HOW DO YOU GET ANY SLEEP ON A MATTRESS MADE OF GOLD? LANCE CAN TELL YOU.
There are enough bits of food in Axl's room to feed most of Knighton.
No way!
The doorbell to my room is a big mace. Isn't it awesome?

THE HOLO TRAINING AREA

PRETTY GREAT, HUH?

This place can simulate anywhere we want.

Can it simulate a cafeteria?

I TAKE A BREAK FROM TRAINING ON THE WEEKENDS. OKAY. I DON'T REALLY.

THE BEST SEQUENCE IS: THRUST. PARRY. PARRY. THRUST. JUMP BACK. RINSE. REPEAT.

ARMORY

EVERY KIND OF WEAPON YOU CAN IMAGINE. E.V.E.R.Y.

Ah, I always feel at home here.

You know how Aaron ties his shoes? In little bows. Get it?

I GET IT. :)

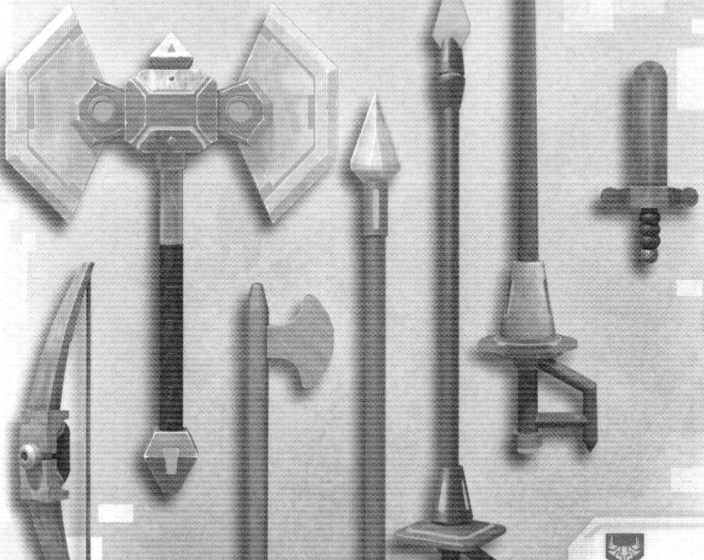

Mom always said, "Never come between a knight and their axe."

KITCHEN AND DINING ROOM

OTHERWISE KNOWN AS AXL'S HQ.

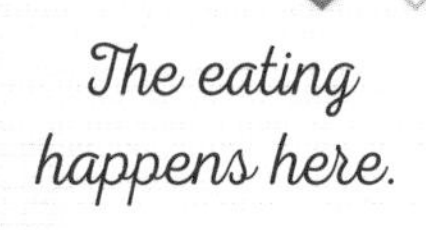

The eating happens here.

Technically your eating happens anywhere!

CHEF ÉCLAIR KEEPS THE KITCHEN VERY NEAT. BUT YOU NEED TO BREAK SOME EGGS TO MAKE AN OMELETTE.

Those pans are potential weapons. They look like flattened maces. :)

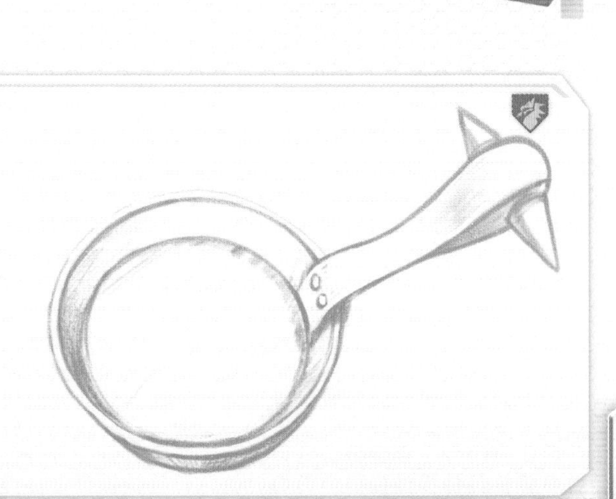

THE LOUNGE

TIME TO RELAX!

Ah . . . Time for some . . . lounging.

YOU SHOULDN'T SPEND MUCH TIME HERE. UNLESS YOU'RE WATCHING SOME TUTORIALS.

My secret move? Grab a snack and a Lancetastic Soda, then take the comfy chair before anyone else does.

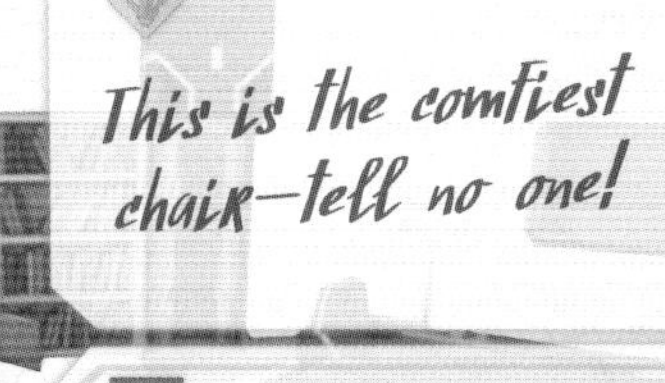

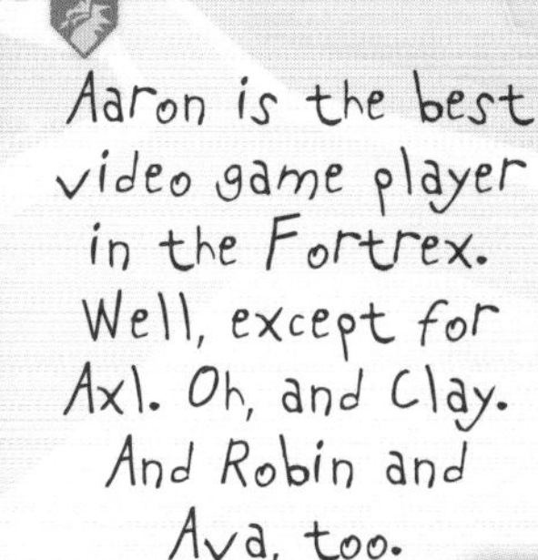

IT'S BIG, LOUD, AND HYPERCHARGED!

Everything here is top secret; so don't tell anyone you saw it. Even me.

TOO LATE, ROBIN. WE SAW IT. :D

Six-speed transmission

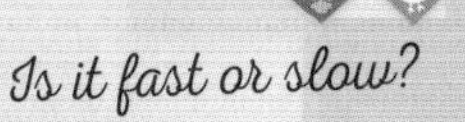

We can get about 50,000 hover horsepower out of this baby.

Gotta change the oil every 5,000 miles.

THE GARAGE

WHERE ALL THE COOL STUFF IS CREATED.

This is the place where I built the Minitrex and the Ultra Armor, as well as my Black Knight Mech.

ALL THE VEHICLES GET PARKED HERE.

Very informative, Clay. If you hadn't of said that we would never have known where to park them. ;)

Wanna see how fast I can change a set of tires or treads?

Should we watch it in slow-mo?

There are about a gazillion screwdrivers in here.

RUMBLE BLADE

BY CLAY MOORINGTON

Built like a giant Claymore Sword, the Rumble Blade is cutting edge in its design and extremely fast. There are two side-cycles that detach and are strong enough to hold someone even as big as Axl. The central sword portion shoots off and becomes a jet-powered flyer, which is perfect for unsuspecting monsters. My Rumble Blade has the perfect service history. That way, I know it is always in impeccable shape and ready for anything.

Wouldn't it be great to have a real sword this big?

Hey, Mr. Gadget, why don't you just make one?

Could Axl really fit in this?

The Rumble Blade has extra energy shooters for anyone sneaking up from behind.

Must remember to never sneak up on Clay!

The cockpit gives me great driving visibility.

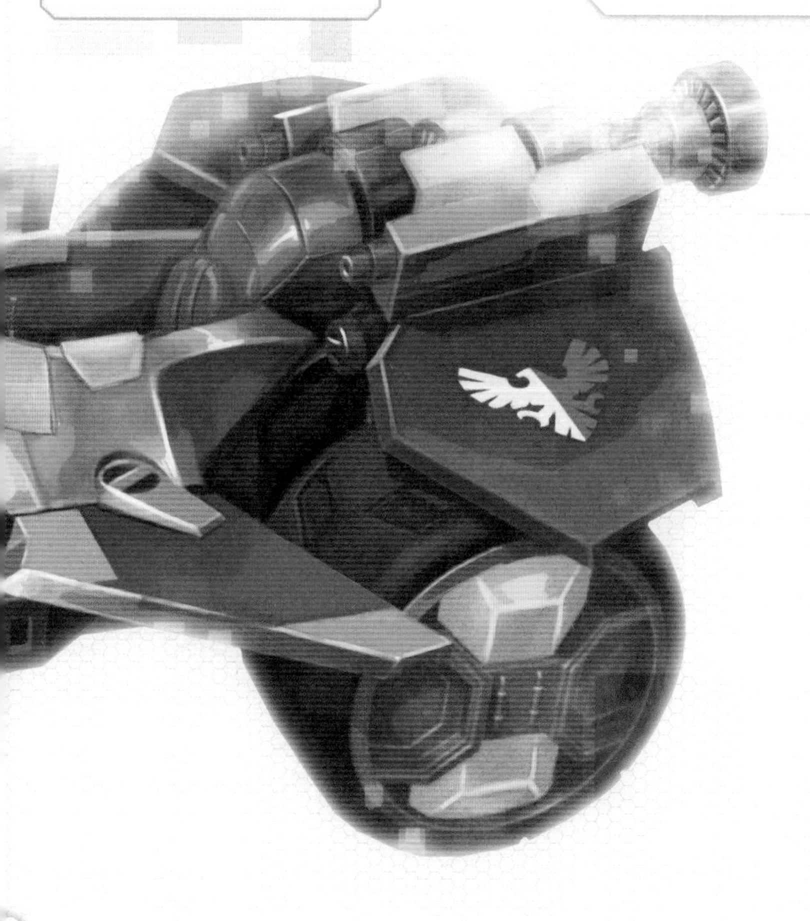

BOW FLYER

BY AARON FOX

Does Aaron ever bow out of a battle?

He doesn't, especially when monsters cross his bows. ;)

Dude, my Bow Flyer can rain down digi-arrows on monsters!

Woo-hoo! Let's take to the skies on my flying Bow Blaster. How cool is this thing? Way cool. It's like a giant bow, only it flies and can shoot energy arrows. There's nothing like takin' down targets or monsters from some altitude.

I'm thinking of repainting it neon green. What do you think?

Always better to be above the action, right?
HEY, THOSE CHAINS REMIND ME OF BEAST MASTER.
Beast Master?! Where?
Sometimes I like to cut the engines and see how far I can glide.

THUNDER MACE

BY MACY HALBERT

I like to call my vehicle the "Mace Masher." That's completely unofficial—don't tell my dad, the King—he's totally into making sure everything is official. It's tough, rugged, and it can mash like the biggest mace you've ever seen. Everything a girl wants in a vehicle.

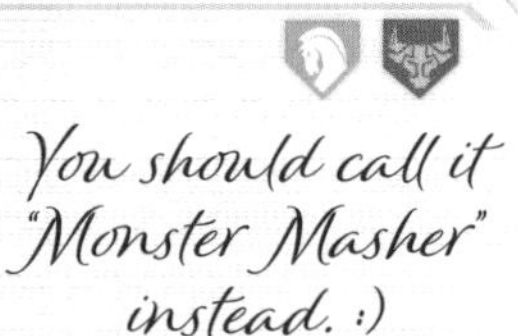

You should call it "Monster Masher" instead. :)

Mmmm, mashed potatoes. I'm so hungry.

Look! My vehicle has a giant, spinning mace!

MACY, WHEN YOU THUNDER PAST THE MONSTERS ON THAT THING, THEY HAVE FACES LIKE THUNDER.

Wow, Clay. You're a real joke masher. ;)

Extra wide tires for grinding across the battlefield

MECHA HORSE

BY LANCE RICHMOND

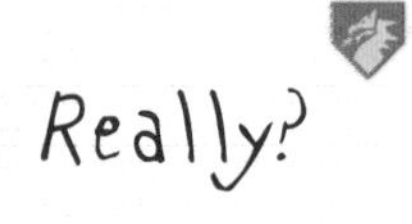

I have the classiest vehicle of all the Knights. It's a classic hover horse named Concordo that converts into a super cycle at the touch of a button. A stylish knight like me requires nothing less. I don't know how it actually works, I just drive around looking good in it. My Mecha Horse is the best because, well, I'm the best.

It's a mecha horse, it's a cycle . . . it's two vehicles in one!

IF YOU CONVERT IT INTO
A HORSE, YOU CAN LOOK JUST
LIKE A KNIGHT FROM THE PAST.

*Yeah, it's perfect
if you happen to be
starring in historical
movies! ;)*

**The steering controls
are solid gold.**

LANCE HAS DENNIS POLISH
THEM EVERY DAY!

*I shine, too, as
I cruise along,
and my hair looks
great with the wind
rushing through it.
(Not too much
though . . . I may
have to go out later.)*

TOWER CARRIER

BY AXL

BRICK: How about, "Be Ready, I Come Keenly"?

Six wheels of ground-poundin' power. Wide and low to the ground for huggin' the road. That part in the back is called the BRICK: Book Repository Integral Containment Keeper. Robin thought up the name and built it in case we ever captured a magic book. That way, there's a safe place to transport it. It's totally awesome!

I customized the seat so my bottom never gets tired.

The **BRICK** is fully detachable if we need to hide it somewhere.

Hey Axl, it looks like a tank. It's nothing compared with the great silhouette of my Mecha Horse.

Yeah, can you tell us which part is the front and which is the back?

You may laugh, but my Tower Carrier is like a surprise waiting to jump out of a giant cake.

Changing six tires takes a lot of time. And with Squirebots helping, it takes twice as long!

THE BLACK KNIGHT

BY ROBIN UNDERWOOD

Sounds awesome! I can totally tutor you in 'not doing anything' if you need me to.

That did say "arrow shooter," right?

The life of a freshman is not cool. All I hear is: "Robin, you can't do this" and "Robin, you can't do that." "You're too young to fight the monsters" and "You're too young to scan the powers."

So if everyone's telling you not to do stuff, what *can* you do to wipe out monsters in the battle against evil? You design cool stuff that can do the job for you! Take a look at my Black Knight—a totally equipped, high-tech mech! Pretty cool, huh? Monsters don't stand a chance against this giant knight, complete with jet-powered boots, gigantic sword, and arrow shooter.

And you know what the most awesome thing about it is? Its ability to hack into the Fortrex for NEXO Power downloads. What's that you say, "You're too young to scan the powers, Robin"? If you did, I didn't hear you! :D

Ava, can you code that so that Merlok can't read it?

No kidding! The Black Knight totally saved the kingdom when Jestro disguised all his monsters as us!

PRINCIPAL BRICKLAND BANNED IT FROM THE KNIGHTS' ACADEMY CAMPUS. AND SNEAKING OUT TO OPERATE IT—EVEN IF IT'S TO SAVE THE KINGDOM—IS STRICTLY PROHIBITED.

I can totally be Robin's "breaking the rules" tutor, if he needs one.

WEAPONS

BY MERLOK 2.0

OBVIOUSLY THE SWORD IS THE BEST WEAPON FOR EVERY SITUATION.

I prefer lots of mashing. Um, I mean macing.

Boo-yah . . . the bow is the only way to go. That rhymes, you know!

I prefer the axe. Well, my name is Axl . . . so it's hardly surprising, is it?

A lance is the weapon of a gentleman and a Richmond. Which is why I'm the only one who can wield it with such grace, elegance, and style.

It's me again (Merlok 2.0, digital wizard and all that). I'm here to . . . what was it again? Oh yes, that's it . . . I'm here to introduce this section on advanced weapons. It has often been said that a NEXO KNIGHTS hero's greatest weapon is his or her mind. Of course, that is if it is a sharp mind! Ha, ha, I said "sharp mind." Get it? Sharp weapon. Sharp mind . . . Never mind . . . Well, anyway, sometimes you just need to hit something really hard with heavy stone and steel—and NEXO Powers, too. For these occasions, personal armaments should be employed.

You have a wide range of amazing, high-tech weapons at your disposal. Of course, each of you will choose what you like best or what works best for you when battling monsters. For example, originally Lance tried to use a bow, but he was hopeless with it, so he discovered that a lance was the weapon for him. It's quite obvious if you think about it, isn't it? So long as the weapon can channel NEXO Powers—which all advanced weapons can—you can choose it for battle.

CLAYMORE SWORD

BY CLAY MOORINGTON

As our mentor Merlok 2.0 said, knights have a wide range of amazing, high-tech weapons to choose from. My choice is a sword. It is the most classic weapon, used by many of the famous knights of Knighton.

The Claymore Sword is a broad sword, which delivers a powerful attack. It can be swung with one hand, but due to its massive size, it is extremely heavy.

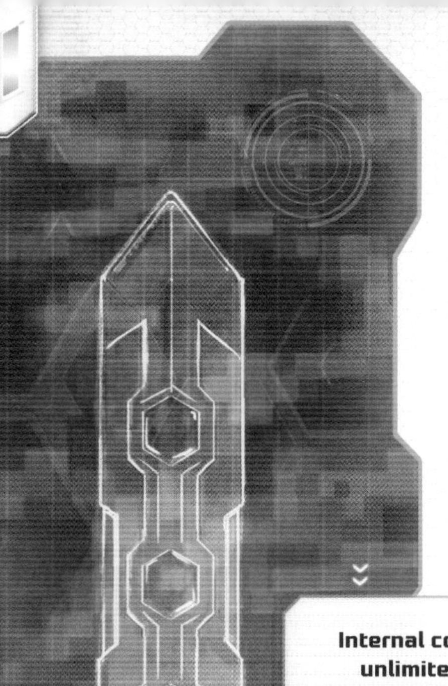

Very sharp. Do not point at your face or you'll poke your eye out.

Blade is made of imperial steel from the south coast of Knighton. This is the strongest known metal in the kingdom.

Ridges carved into blade provide high-speed transport channels for energy.

Internal core in cross guard offers unlimited storage capacity for NEXO Power downloads.

Handle grip is wrapped in wolf leather and gryphon skin.

Size Comparison

Claymore Sword

Normal Sword

Pommel is best for cracking walnuts, but don't ever let Clay see you use it for that.

My lance is even bigger. And shinier.

BLAZER BOW

BY AARON FOX

Yeah, I tried this one and I must say it's overrated.

A bad workman always blames his tools.

I would never blame my tools. They are sooo cool.

Want to defeat monsters and quick? My crossbow can fire an almost infinite supply of digi-arrows—a highly charged, shaft-like burst of energy. Wow! Can you feel the power? Oh, yeah! Bows are the grooviest weapons in Knighton, so if you need to strike at a monster from any kind of distance, you know what to choose. Combine it with hover-shield riding and the Blazer Bow is the best of the best, dude!

Muzzle coated in liquid Spurion to enhance speed and force of digi-arrows.

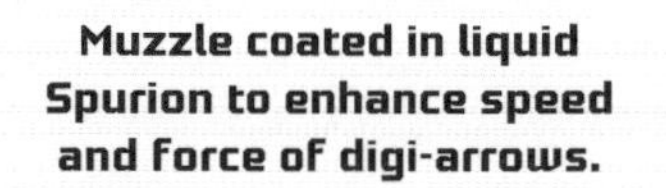

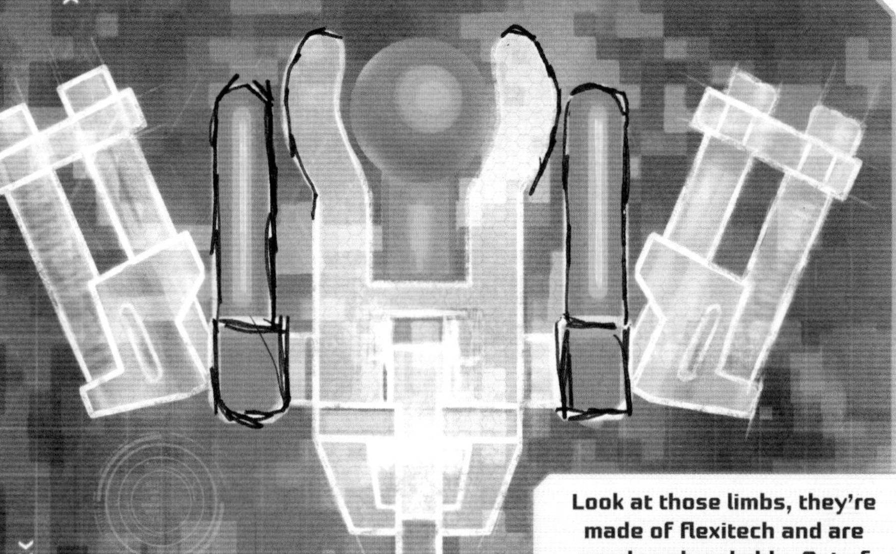

Look at those limbs, they're made of flexitech and are nearly unbreakable. Out of this world!

Barrel holds and produces up to seventy digi-arrows per minute. Great result, huh?

ACTUALLY. THEY ARE NOT OUT OF THIS WORLD. THEY ARE CARVED FROM A SYNTHETIC MATERIAL THAT NOW GROWS WILD IN THE FORESTS OF KNIGHTON.

Only a small squeeze of a pistol grip and you rapid-fire a rain of digi-arrows. Monsters, beware!

Are you serious, Clay?

I'm afraid he is. :D

THE LANCE

BY LANCE RICHMOND

If you want your weapon to not only be effective but striking as well, choose the lance. Of course, yours won't be as glamorous as mine (it's a Richmond's lance) but it will definitely be better than any bow.

My lance is both lightweight and strong. And it's elegant, just like me! Robin told me it has an <u>internal carton</u> providing high-speed processing of energy normally not seen in weapons of this type. You see, Aaron, not only your bow bursts energy!

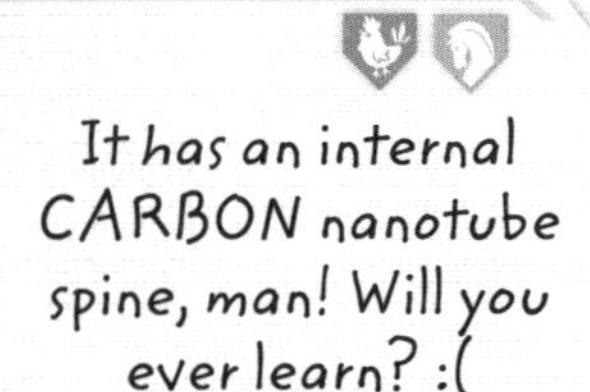

Hey, Lance, Squirerazzi!

Where?

I was kidding. But you're striking when you strike a pose! ;P

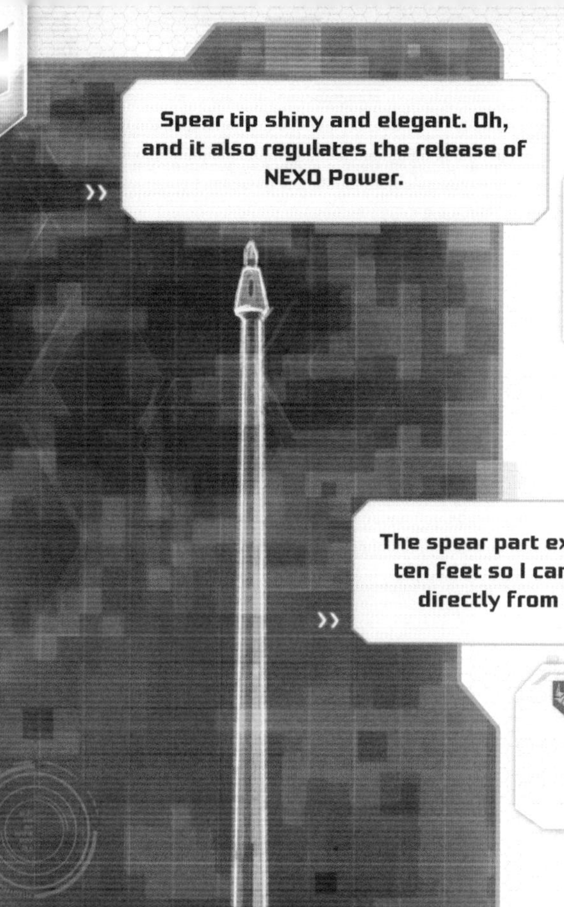

Spear tip shiny and elegant. Oh, and it also regulates the release of NEXO Power.

But you're still trying to use it for picking my nose. Not funny!

The spear part extends more than ten feet so I can pick a monster directly from my hammock.

Could you please pick me up a sausage, too?

Don't tell anyone, but there's a secret pocket inside the handle.

For carrying spare change and fan mail, no doubt! :)

PHOTON MACE

BY MACY HALBERT

I must admit, your mace has a surprising elegance and charm.

Thanks, Lance, I know that was hard for you to admit.

Some narrow-minded people say that weapons aren't really for girls. They are sooo wrong! What about Joan of Dark or Catherine of Dragon? They wielded their weapons with such grace. My mom, Queen Halbert, who comes from a long line of mace-wielding warriors, gave me my beloved Photon Mace. Why is it called a Photon Mace? Well, put simply, it packs the power of the sun when I swing it! Look out, monsters, here I come!

Head carved from solarantium stone—an extremely rare and indestructible material that is believed to have originated on the surface of the sun

So, can we call you a Sun Warrior, Macy?

Yeah, you'd better grab a shield and some SPF fifty when I'm in action!

Handle is made from the silicon-infused tusk of an angry woolly mammoth. And if you've ever tried to get a bunch of silicon into an angry mammoth's tusk, you'd be really impressed by that.

I THOUGHT THAT MAMMOTHS WERE EXTINCT . . .

Spare energy is stored in a special reservoir at the base of the handle, so I have a secret pocket, too.

BIG POWER AXE

BY AXL

Strikes to monsters or to fried chickens? ;D

So big and so sensitive, oh . . .

Ehhh, what can I say? A weapon is a weapon. It should be practical and deliver devastating strikes. My axe was forged from riches found only in my land: hyper-iron from the Deep Earth mines and wood from the Old Growth Ironwood Tree. It is strong and big just like me. North Hill Country, I miss you so much. :'(

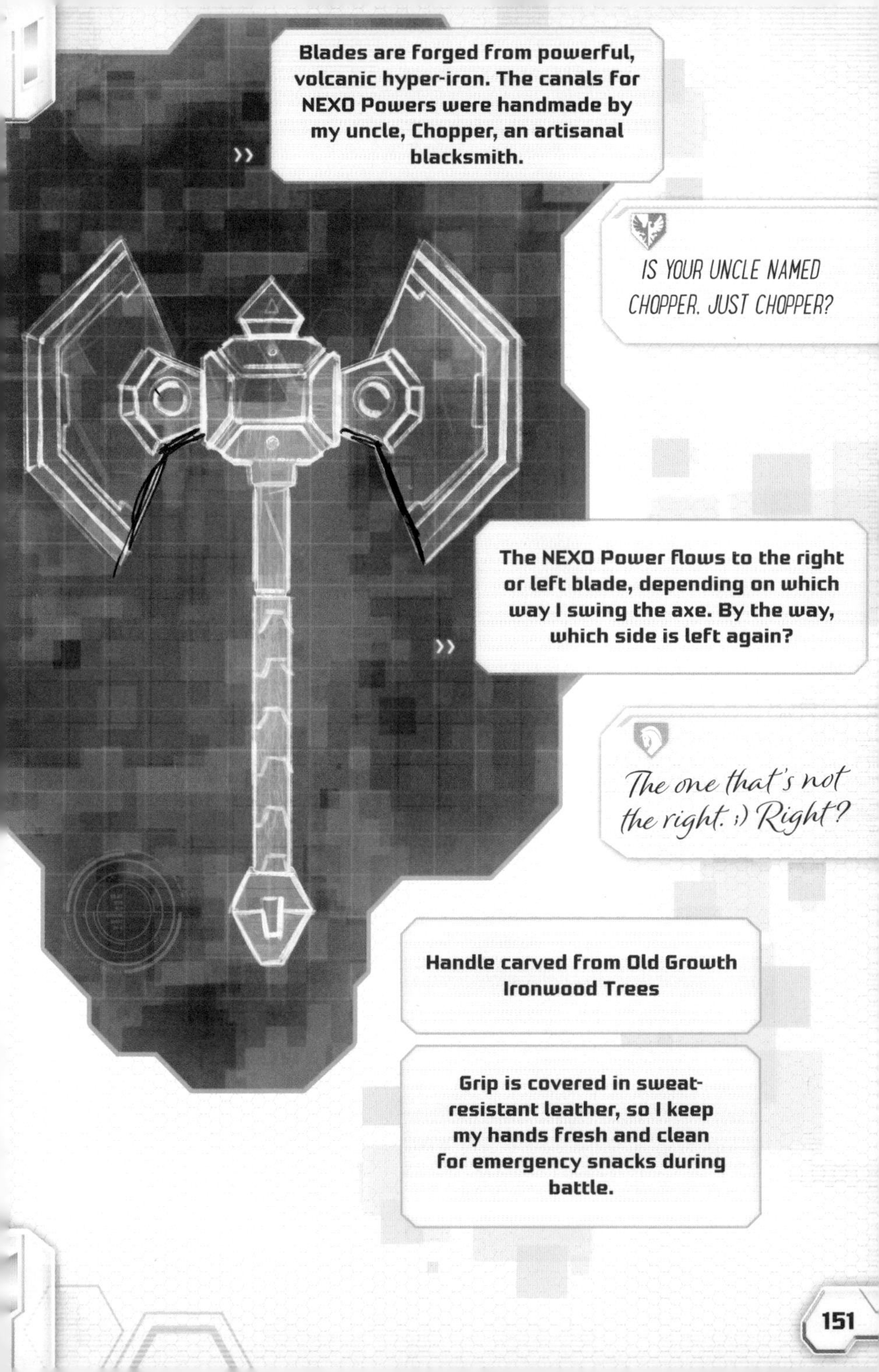
Blades are forged from powerful, volcanic hyper-iron. The canals for NEXO Powers were handmade by my uncle, Chopper, an artisanal blacksmith.
IS YOUR UNCLE NAMED CHOPPER. JUST CHOPPER?
The NEXO Power flows to the right or left blade, depending on which way I swing the axe. By the way, which side is left again?
The one that's not the right. ;) Right?
Handle carved from Old Growth Ironwood Trees
Grip is covered in sweat-resistant leather, so I keep my hands fresh and clean for emergency snacks during battle.

JESTRO AND THE BOOK OF MONSTERS

BY MERLOK 2.0

So you have great weapons, now you need some enemies, right? Meet grumpy Jestro and The Book of Monsters. Odd couples don't get as odd or as evil as the former royal jester and his magical minion. The Book of Monsters seems like he's really calling the shots, but then again he can't go anywhere other than the local library, without his jokey compatriot.

Why didn't he like my place? I don't know . . . Maybe it was because I didn't let him take over the kingdom and I put him up on a dusty shelf . . .? Well, now he's free with a little help from Jestro. They're two crazy guys trying to lead a team of Lava, Forest, and Sea Monsters. But we are ready, aren't we, NEXO KNIGHTS! Erm . . . aren't we?

"Magical minion"! Ha, ha, ha!

If The Book of Monsters heard that, he would need to eat The Knight's Book of Calm.

I didn't know that book existed . . . Does it exist?

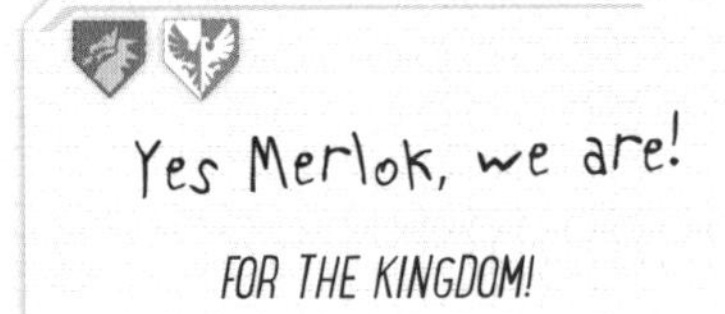

Yes Merlok, we are!

FOR THE KINGDOM!

LAVA MONSTERS

"Hot, nasty, fiery, and really unfriendly" pretty much sums up the Lava Monsters faced by our team. There are generals like Magmar and lieutenants, like Beast Master and Lavaria. Then there are the common, everyday Magma Monsters: Scurriers, Globlins, and Bloblins who'll melt you just like the others. Too many to remember? Just take a look around and search for something red and stinky.

Don't forget Lava Beetle, Fire Scorpion, and Storm Eye.

Yeah, they rock! (Lava rock.)

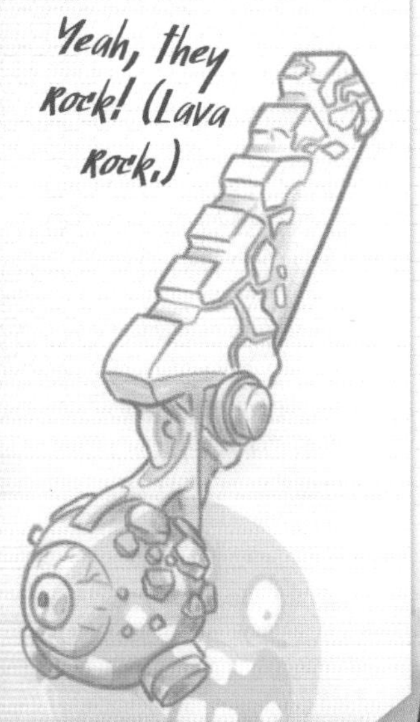

Hey, what's the difference between a Globlin and a rolling lava rock?

None. Ha, ha, ha!

LAVARIA—JESTRO'S CHIEF SPY AND MISTRESS OF DISGUISE.

Whiparella—she can spread fear with a SNAP of her nasty whips.
You know I'm fearless. Erm . . . almost.
You know that one of Monster Master's Globlins is named Muffin? Sweet . . .
DON'T EVER TRY TO EAT HIM, AXL.
Too late ;)

SEA MONSTERS

So, er, was that all too hot for you? I think it must be time to cool down a bit with the cold and wet Sea Monsters. It's always best to be aware of them if you're near any type of water. If you're out at sea, look for pirate ships fuelled by electric eels. If you're staying on an island, you'd better check whether it has tentacles beneath it as well as palm trees on top. If you're crossing a moat . . . um, what was this one again? Oh yes, that's right. If you're crossing a moat, be sure to look down so that Sharkerado doesn't surprise you! That reminds me . . . Robin, we need to talk about the water-resistant armor for the Knights.

I always wanted to meet Chef Savage and read his Cookbook of Evil.

Must chefs always have a French surname?

The Siren of Seaguard won Lava Lands Idol last year. Girl power!
Can you watch it on KnighTube?
Yes, but only the karaoke version. :P

FOREST MONSTERS

Merlok, you are a hologram now . . .

Being close to nature is something I would not recommend when in the presence of the Forest Monsters. A close hug from Bramblina or a bite of the poisoned apple from Baron Badwood will soon make you wish you had stayed at home. *Achoo!* Yikes, is that my allergy from the Strom of Spores made by Mushlord the Marauder? Heeelp!

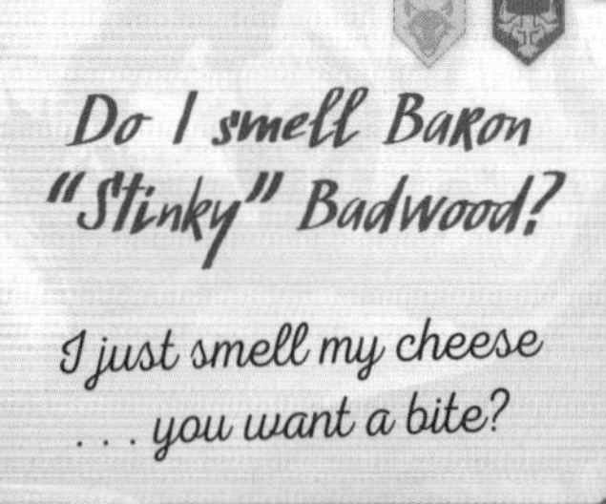

Hey, which one is Deadwood and which one is (K)not?
–KNOCK, KNOCK!
–WHO'S THERE?
–A CRANKY WOODPECKER :)

THE EVIL MOBILE

It's kinda nutty, but the Evil Mobile is faster than it looks.

As they say in the fashion news, it's hot, hot, hot!

WE MUST STUDY THIS VEHICLE AND KNOW OUR ENEMY.

Wow. Did you really just say, "know our enemy?" I think you need a rewrite!

Even bad guys need a good ride, and Jestro has one—the Evil Mobile. It's big, bad, and a bit of a mess, really. But that's what happens when you have Beast Master and his Chaos Monsters build you a vehicle.

How do you recognize it when you pass it? Well, it looks just like Jestro. It has a jester's hat and jaws with enormous teeth. And huge wheels. And a catapult to launch lava rocks. And a movable cockpit . . . You get the idea.

And it's pulled by Burnzie and Sparkks, so it gets at least two monsters to the mile. Also, Globlins jump in and power the wheels when they need a bit of a boost.

Those guys must get hungry pulling that thing everywhere.

It's not very high-tech. Actually, it's not high-tech at all.
And it's got no air conditioning.
These Globlin-throwing catapults are dangerous. I know all too well!
Lava rock wheels make for a bumpy ride.
I'm glad it doesn't fly.

TRACKING MONSTERS

One of the most important skills you must learn is how to locate the monsters threatening the security of our kingdom. Of course, you can find them in The Book of Monsters, but when released, all evil creatures leave different trails. Here's how to identify and track the markings of these dangerous foes.

SCURRIERS
The rodents of the monster world. Their footprints are small but very stinky. Prone to distraction, they rarely walk in a straight line.

Awww, their feet are so tiny.

Oh, rodents. I always wanted to have a guinea pig. :)

GLOBLINS

Globlins don't actually have feet so it's hard to find their footprints. But they still leave a trail—sort of like a beach ball made of lava bouncing across the countryside.

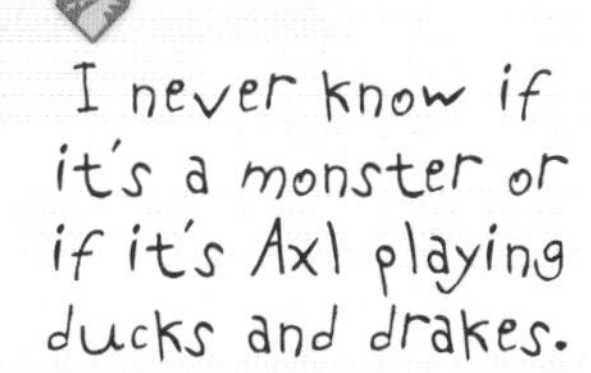

UNDERWATER MONSTERS

Some monsters never surface. If you see circles in the water, avoid diving in.

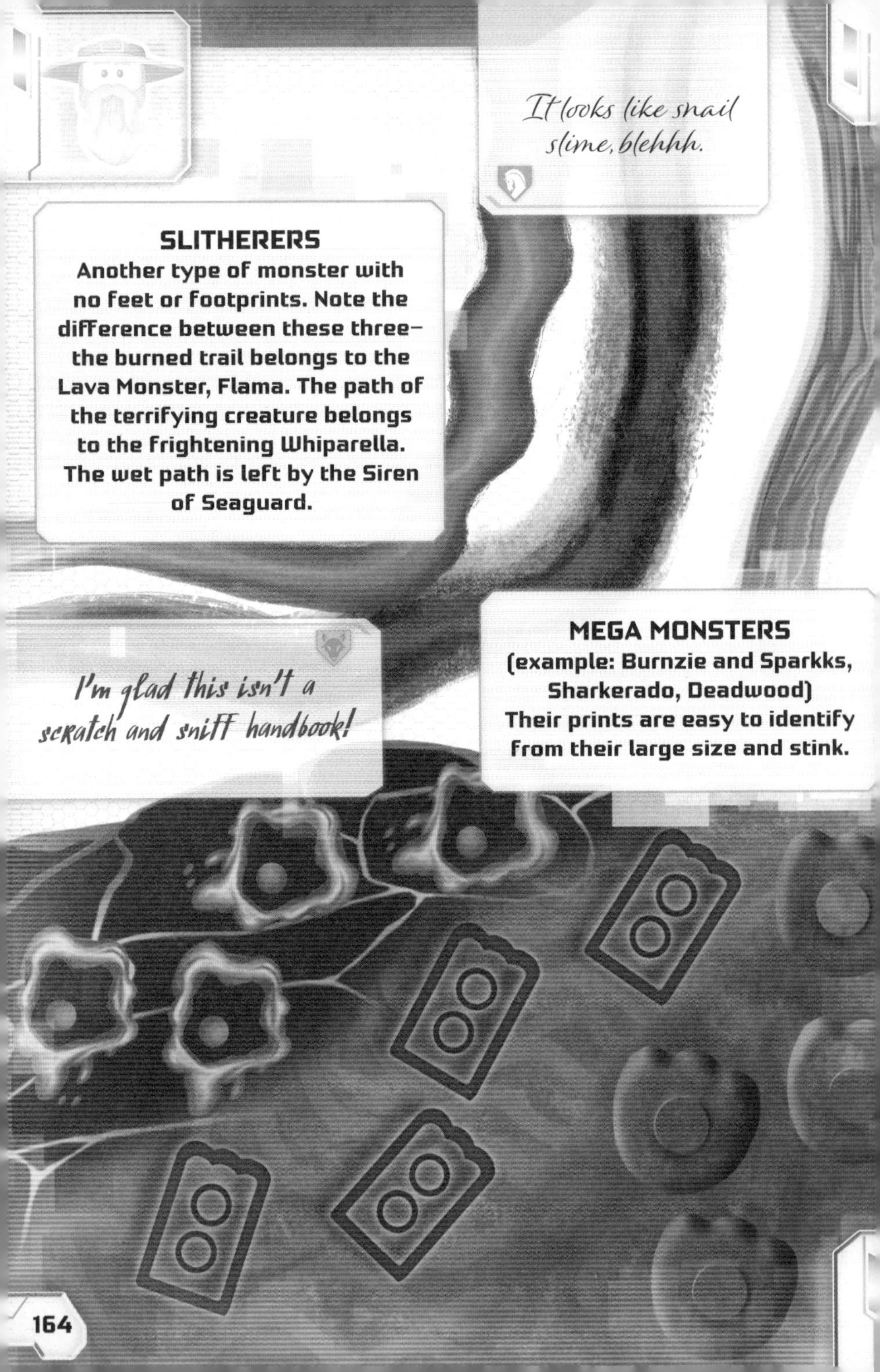
It looks like snail slime, blehhh.
SLITHERERS
Another type of monster with no feet or footprints. Note the difference between these three–the burned trail belongs to the Lava Monster, Flama. The path of the terrifying creature belongs to the frightening Whiparella. The wet path is left by the Siren of Seaguard.
I'm glad this isn't a scratch and sniff handbook!
MEGA MONSTERS
(example: Burnzie and Sparkks, Sharkerado, Deadwood)
Their prints are easy to identify from their large size and stink.

MONSTER IN DISGUISE

These may look like dog prints, but they are actually the prints of Lavaria, who not only disguises her body, but her footprints as well.

Hey, did anyone ever find that lost dog? Oh wait . . . It's Lavaria.

OTHER MONSTERS

Most normal monsters will leave a footprint similar to a human, but with burnt, wet, or muddy edges.

Are there ANY normal monsters?

FIGHTING TIPS

BY CLAY MOORINGTON

That's a fancy way of saying, "You mess with us and we'll go all 'medieval' on you!"

A knight's goal in combat is never to cause unnecessary harm or suffering to an opponent. His or her only goal is to provide a proper physical deterrent to ensure the protection of the kingdom. This deterrent takes many forms. Below is a list of some of the most common defensive activities.

The best defense is a good offense, right guys?

Scare them away! I can do that.

1. An overwhelming show of force

An axe works for me!

2. Repeated strikes with a sharp or blunt object

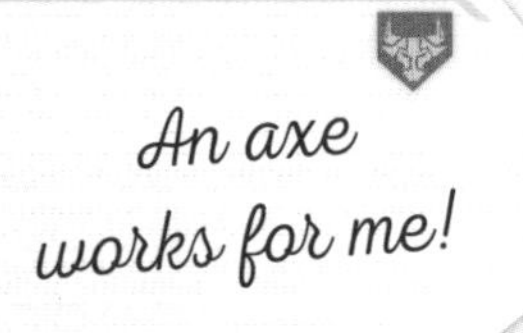

Hello, digi-bow!

3. Disruption with projectiles

Hello, dirty tricks!

4. Tactical sabotage

Prepare for an upload!

5. NEXO Powers

Always remember that you are not just defending the kingdom, you are representing its spirit and its future. Crush your opponents, but do it with honor and style.

HIDING AND MASKING

Fighting monsters is more complicated than anyone ever expects it to be. Monsters are extremely powerful and possess many heightened senses. A successful knight must be prepared to attack these creatures using effective stealth and flawless camouflage.

Below are some helpful tips for sneaking up on your monster opponent.

What about snacks? Can they smell those, too?

1. Brush your teeth. Monsters can smell your last meal from a mile off.

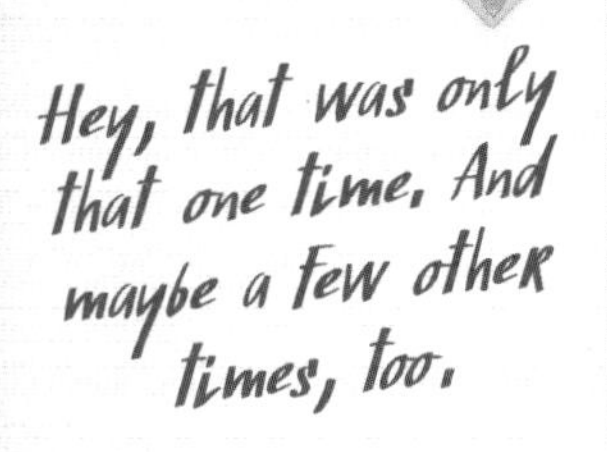

2. Avoid singing, whistling, or humming. Seems obvious, but you'd be surprised at how many knights hum their own theme song whilst attacking.

Or two . . .
Or more . . .

3. **Everyone loves a snappy catchphrase, so prepare one to use after you win the battle.**

I couldn't help it! The battle boots clashed with my gown!

Ironic as always, Macy. Love it!

4. **Avoid wearing high heels during surprise attacks.**

Sorry, you'll have to talk to my personal publicity Squirebot about that—he promotes and approves all my sneak attacks.

5. **And no personal publicity Squirebots on secret missions.**

TEAM MISSIONS–

WHAT'S IMPORTANT?

Finally, some advice about fighting as a NEXO KNIGHTS hero, a member of an elite team sworn to protect the kingdom of Knighton from all monster threats. They may not always agree, but they'll always be teammates!

There is an I in Tiim: T.i.i.m. Man, can't you spell?!

CLAY: The Knight's Code and our experience as students at the Knights' Academy guide our every move on the battlefield. There is no "I" in "team." But there is an "e" in "we". And it takes all of "we" to work to our utmost to protect the kingdom and fight for justice and chivalry.

MACY: Wow, what can I say? I'd be nothing without those other fabulous NEXO KNIGHTS heroes around me. Even Lance. They make me the best mace-wielding princess that ever was. And even though sometimes we don't agree about strategy, I think we do all agree that we couldn't do what we do without everybody pitching in.

AXL: Hey, the team has always got my back. I was from a little town in the Hill Country, and they all made me feel special and part of the group. Sure, lots of times I gotta do the heavy lifting, but that's how I contribute to the team. Always remember: You do what you can and you try your best. That makes you a good teammate.

AARON: Check it—I'm the knight who always pushes the team in gnarly new directions. Don't be afraid to think out of the box. Or, like, totally destroy the box and fly off on your shield! Look, I used to be all about pushing myself and doing crazy stunts all on my own. Not any more. Now it's about doing crazy things to help the team. What an off-the-shield thought is that, yo?

Lance!
How would you like a Flying Macy on your backside!

LANCE: The one thing that really makes this team function is . . . me. The rest of the NEXO KNIGHTS heroes fill <u>supporting roles</u>. They're adequate. Yes, that's the word . . .

LANCE: Fine, fine! If you want to know the real truth, I'm pretty, pretty, pretty lucky to have these other knights with me. Sure, they don't have great taste in hair-care products, but they are, well, they're great. <u>They're always there for me</u>. Okay, that felt good to say. Now, off to the Knight Club . . .

Remember how we all started on that tournament team at the Knights' Academy?

Good times, big guy. Good times!

TEAMWORK

Clay Moorington here with a few final thoughts on teamwork. Teamwork isn't just a thing . . . it's the ONLY thing. Without teamwork, the NEXO KNIGHTS heroes would be a disjointed, unruly, disorganized band of folk, tripping over themselves while holding pointy things. It would never work. But when we give up our own personal needs and desires to help the group succeed, well, we actually find that we always meet our own goals, too. Our team is amazing, strong, and powerful. Though I think of myself as a true keeper of *The Knight's Code*, my fantastic teammates always show me new ways to live up to the code. Don't let them hear me say it, but I really love those guys!

Yo, Clay-man . . . I heard that! Love you, too, bro!

Teamwork IS the most important thing.
(Other than lunch. And dinner. Oh, and breakfast.)

Let's face it, we wouldn't even be a team without Clay!

Clay is the only one I've met who comes close to living up to my high standards. Especially with a sword. That guy's always cleaving stuff.

WHAT THE CODE MEANS TO ME

All knights should be aware of what the Knight's Code means to them. Especially us, NEXO KNIGHTS heroes, we must be ready to face the danger and defend our king and our people.

This is what it means to us . . .

THE CODE IS EVERYTHING TO ME. I'M NOT SURE HOW TO BE MORE SPECIFIC THAN THAT. IT RULES MY LIFE, MY THOUGHTS, AND MY ACTIONS. AS THE CODE SAYS, "I AM THE CODE. THE CODE IS ME." WELL, IT DOESN'T ACTUALLY SAY THAT. BUT IT SHOULD—CLAY

Yes, like Clay says, the Knight's Code is important. But you know what's really important when you're a knight? Looking awesome. And that's something I do really well. Sure, you can be all noble and heroic, but no one will remember you unless you're rockin' some shiny armor and an even shinier smile. So don't just follow the Code, set the trend. Save the kingdom, but do it with style. That's the Code according to Lance Richmond.

It's nowhere near as much fun sticking notes in this book when they actually ask you to do it. So I'll keep this short. The Code is cool. Enough said. Aaron out.

I believe in the Code. I believe in our kingdom. But I also believe we need to be more flexible. This is a complex world and 200 words written a few centuries ago may not have the answer to every single problem we're going to face in modern times. The Code is an excellent place to start, but I look at it more like this: The Code will guide us, but it does not have to command us. —Macy

The Code makes sense to me. When I first got into the academy, I memorized the Code by writing its words in icing on my favorite cake. And then I ate the cake. It's kind of weird though; every time I think of the Code now, I get really hungry. Some people think the Code is everything. I think it's a deliciously sweet and frosted cake. But that's just me. – Axl

THE END. OR JUST THE BEGINNING?

So, are we finished? ;)

I'm guessing the monsters are "finished" now that everyone's read this book. :P

THE MONSTERS ARE NOT FINISHED YET. SO REMEMBER WHAT YOU'VE LEARNT AND ALWAYS BE VIRTUOUS, WORTHY, AND TRULY GREAT KNIGHTS.

Axl is the greatest one. :D

And you're still in pretty good shape, Clay! :)

ERM . . . SO AFTER READING THIS HANDBOOK YOU SHOULD NOW KNOW EVERYTHING . . .

I still don't know how to fit my hair under my helmet without messing it up. ;)

Or how many cakes to eat before battle.

Or how many times Clay has read this book. :P

Or . . .

Sorry, guys, I need to stop your chat.
I think we have some company.

Preparing NEXO POWERS!

POWER OF UNIIIITED KNIIIIGHTS!

NEXOOO KNIGHTS!